10655926

The Faces of Blood Kindred

Books by William Goyen

The Faces of Blood Kindred
In a Farther Country
Ghost and Flesh
The House of Breath

THE FACES OF BLOOD KINDRED

A Novella and Ten Stories

by

William

GOYEN

Random House

First Printing

 Published in New York by Random House, Inc., and simultaneously in Toronto, Canada, by Random House of Canada, Limited.

Library of Congress Catalog Card Number: 60–12124

Manufactured in the United States of America

by George McKibbin & Son

For Joe
and May

Contents

The Faces of Blood Kindred

Savata, My Fair Sister

All the rest of us in our family are dark; but Savata my sister is fair. Now Jesus, did you know, was himself a dark man. They say his hair was like lamb's wool and his feet like polished brass. Thank you Jesus.

Being fair-complected, my sister Savata has always felt outcast from the rest of us dark ones in the family. I saw this psychology of her early when it put her on the wrong track by driving her away to sing and dance in St. Louis. I wrote to her and said, Savata you are feeling apart; do not; you are blessed and set aside by Jesus. See it thataway; you are marked for special work for our Lord and Savior. Come on up here to Philadelphia where I am and work with Daddy Grace, he will put your fairness to uses of the Lord and His Name. Savata had a singing voice which Jesus blessed her with, thank you Jesus, I had not much of one but gave what I had of it to the Church.

Savata to my surprise came in her fairness to Philadelphia and lent her talent to Daddy Grace. He said he was just borrowing it for the Lord who would return it to her twofold. Well, Savata studied diction and delivery, she studied Hebrew (for we are Black Jews by ancestry), she changed her personality, got all of that baseness out of her system; and in time she got her preaching papers. There is a lot of money, oh a lot of money in God's Church. Savata, my fair sister, and I came to Brooklyn and established the Light of the World Holiness Church. She was ordained a Bishop and I was appointed by her to be her business manager. The Bishop Savata worked hard, Savata sang and Savata preached and I went door to door asking donations for our church. Savata grew more beautiful and more fair. She drew larger and larger crowds, more and more donations. People came from all over to hear and see such a fair Bishop. Many gave as much as $15 per Sunday. Then this little person appeared on our scene.

His name was Canaan Johnson and he was, I will have to admit, a smart thing. He knew Hebrew but was studying it even further; he was a teacher, black as the ace of spades, and asked Savata to set him up as a teacher of Hebrew to the members of the L.O.W. H.C. As we are the Black Jews by our ancestry, Savata announced to her congregation that Canaan Johnson would be at the disposal of them for $1.25 an hour as a teacher of Hebrew, which all must learn, to get the true tongue of Jesus, to be rightly saved. You can't be truly saved in just translation, Canaan Johnson announced to the congregation. Naturally they were all scrambling to him with their $1.25 an hour. Before I knew it Savata had not only taken him as a boarder into her house which the church bought for her as a Bishop's Lodgings, but had appointed *him* business manager of the Light of the World Holiness Church. The next thing we knew he had done disbursed $600 for a piano, $3000 for a pipe organ, and $100 for something we could never find out. I kept quiet (thank you Jesus) and withdrew from Savata's church. I put away my preaching papers and housecleaned for a living. Savata never made attempt once to get in touch with me. I sure had to pray hard to keep religion, I honestly tell you.

All while I was cleaning house, all while I was vacuuming and apolishing, I studied this situation and I was delivering one long livid sermon to Canaan Johnson, no doubt my masterpiece if it could have been heard. I would not go near to the church except to clean it on Saturdays. I owed this to the Lord and it was not for Savata and Canaan Johnson; it was my tithe. This is how I heard things. Savata had changed radically. She owned more and more possessions. She preached in a streamlined dress of silk and on it she wore a diamond star, I heard. It was her fairness's fault, I said. As we are the Black Jews, her difference became her curse, where she could have made it her blessing. Look how some other handicapped folks do—that Mordecai Blake, he scuffles himself, sitting down, all over the sidewalks of Great Neck in the name of the Church, and gets more contributions than a man with good legs awalking.

Time passed, with me housecleaning and tithing my time to the L.O.W.H.C. on Saturdays and hearing things and studying what to do. I kept my feelings to myself, thank you Jesus. Until one day I was told by the Lord to go visit Savata and to reason out with her, to try to help her. I went to her house in Brooklyn and what did I find but good Persian rugs on the floor, new slip covers on the furniture and I don't know what all else. Savata, I said, I hear you have a cluster of diamonds shape of the Star of David and a Persian lamb coat, added to all the rest of this display. Where Savata had before a deep voice for preaching and for singing, she now had a little pussy voice that made me sick at my stomach. She was put-on from head to toe, and it was the working of Mr. Canaan Johnson, believe you me. Savata, my fair sister, I said, your voice has done changed, your hair has changed in color toward the red side, I cannot believe you are my same sister. Let your sister look you over. Savata would not look me in the eye. You will not look your sister in the eye, I said, but you will scan *her* over to a T to see how stout she is because of her diabetes and to see the varicose veins in her legs from carrying too much weight. I am still in the service of the Lord, despite my personal appearance, I told her that. Savata said I ate too much cream things. To this I said right out, Savata let your sister see your diamonds and your Persian lamb.

Savata was stand-offish about it and said she did not display her private possessions openly. She said she wore them only around the house. This is around the house, I said, so let me see you in them. I hear tell you blind your congregation with the diamond cluster on Sundays—let it shed a little of its light on your poor sister. She purred and said Canaan Johnson would not like her to display her things openly. How close can you get, I queried her—in a room with your own flesh and blood kin? Savata prissed and said we had different fathers and I knew it. Now how uncharitable can you get?

Then I had to let go and tell Savata my true feelings, as the Lord had instructed me to if pressed, and for her good. I said, Savata you are a Daughter of Babylon and you know what that is. That man Canaan Johnson is laying up all day studying up while you're out working. He's bound to get the best of you in the end, if he hasn't already. You're *paying* him to, I said. He is the Devil Incarnit. Will you please listen to your sister that you used to look for creesy-greens with in the marshes to make poke salad, that you walked barefooted with in the meadows, singing to Jesus. Remember your mother who raised you up under the apple trees. If you do not remember the days of your youth then may your tongue cleave to the roof of your mouth. We will discard the fact that you ran off to Montgomery and danced in the Sepia Revue of 1952 and remember only that I rescued you up to Philadelphia and saved your soul and put you on the right track. Do not backslide. Oh I told her. You are the fair one, I said, and you are marked off to do a special service by Jesus, and you are just having the wool pulled over your eyes by this studying man. He is smart, I grant you that, and knows Hebrew and studies up all day in his room; but he is studying up, at your expense, to leave you in the end; and pocket all your earnings in his pocket. Savata only whined back *uh-huh* in that ungodly Lana Turner voice. But I went on.

I said you must withdraw him as business manager of the church and reinstate me before all is lost to the Devil. I have had to go back to housecleaning because I have withdrawn myself from the Church. My papers are laying dormant in my bureau drawer, but they are up to date. You know I am overweight and have sugar-poisoning to boot. Savata my sister that the Lord blessed, I said, will you listen to me? But Savata stood calm and cold before me with her arms in a prissy position as if she was embracing herself . . . what that man Canaan Johnson had put into her, among other things, though he was very bright, granted. I got up to leave and said, Savata you are the fairest of us all and yet have the most talents: with the most talents come the most temptations, I know that. And I know that Daddy Grace promised your talent would be turned back onto you twofold if you gave it to the Lord, and that instead your temptation has been doubled on you—never mind. Listen to me, you have just that much more to preach about—more temptations. Do you think Jesus' disciples were spared temptations? Before I go, though, I would like to ask you one simple temptation and that is to have the courage to put on your lamb's wool coat for your diabetic sister and ex-business manager of the Light of the World Holiness Church to see you in it; and pin on your cluster of diamonds.

To my surprise she left the room and came back in her things. She stood before me in her coat that looked like they say the hair of Jesus was. I was impressed: she was a sight; almost, I thought, too physical to be a Bishop. Maybe I had put Savata on the wrong track. I made her take off her shoes and stockings and stand barefooted before me the way nature and God had made her, before Canaan Johnson shod her with brazen slippers. She did not have the legs for a Bishop, that was plain to see. I began to sing softly "Just As I Am Without One Plea." And to my joy—and thank you Jesus—I heard in a short time the sweet voice of Savata, pure and fair, singing the alto with me, standing barefooted with feet of polished brass and in her hair-of-Jesus Persian lamb and with her diamond cluster atwinkling. She looked like a Saint, her fair face aglow, the Jesus hair of the coat ashining and her cluster aburst with light, in that blessed moment; and I knew that she was still possible, despite her physical make-up, and that more than ever, even more than back in 1952 when she got off on the wrong track, it was my Divine God's business to save her back and steer her right again. The thing of it was, you had to lead Savata, show her where to go; she would run with the fox or chase with the hounds, either way, you just had to watch her all the time: a bad nature for a Bishop. Still, she had drawing power.

In suddenly walked Canaan Johnson with some deep book in his hand, and you could tell by the back of his head how he had been reading it, flat on his back. He had on a velvet smoking jacket. Savata stopped her singing and pursed her lips and said, *Ca-na-a-an;* but I went on . . . "Oh Lamb of Jesus I come, I come . . ."

Canaan Johnson sat down with his finger in his book and Savata sat down. When I finished singing, Canaan Johnson said, God bless you Ruby Drew for giving your voice to the Lord, and shot a glance at Savata. I said it is given free of charge to all who will hear it like the wind that doth blow, Canaan Johnson, I charge no fee for it; and looked him straight in his eye. If I should ask a price for what I give, I could have new slip covers too and a house with five rooms and a coat and a diamond cluster. The word of God, translated or no, does not reward us *all* with a velvet smoking jacket. I would be satisfied if it blessed me with just a pair of Denver heels on these old shoes. And if it would allow me a down payment of $5.00 on a refrigerator to save me from carrying ice up four flights to keep my husband's milk from souring. I am a Minister of the Gospel and have the papers to prove it.

Now, Ruby, he said in that voice, the source of your rancor is about the business manager of the Light of the World Holiness Church. This is obvious. The change has been hard on you but it has brought a great improvement in the Bishop Savata's church. Already the membership has been increased twofold and we are only beginning. It is a man's job to business manage a church.

I see what you mean, I said, snapping him and casting an eye over Savata who had put back on her boa boudoir slippers. You have disbursed $3000 of the church's funds for a pipe organ without one pipe organist to play it. The piano was ample enough, yet you had to replace it by a new one which you disbursed out $600 for from the funds of the church. You have robed my sister Savata in lamb's wool and displayed a diamond star cluster upon her breast and covered her furniture with new chintz and put down new rugs upon her floors, all in a new house that was disbursed for out of the church's funds, man's job or none.

For income-tax purposes, Canaan Johnson put in; but I cut right through that by asking him: as I am my sister's guardian, I have come here to ask what are your plans, Canaan Johnson, and how far are you going with this thing?

My plans are to serve the Lord through the instrument of Savata, he responded.

She is not your instrument, I said. You are playing with a Bishop of Jesus, camouflaging her to look like the Whore of Babylon, and all on the church's funds. In the hands of some men, natural God-made beauty is turned into a false idol. I said haven't you found yourself a good thing! Oh I know, I said. Behind all the downfalls of good great women stands an attractive man with presents and lies and private notions. Not a humpback, not a big-eared plain man or a serious settled type, but a jazzy, good-looking oily one with voice of a dove and tongue of a serpent . . .

You are so plainly after the Bishopric, Ruby Drew, Canaan Johnson said, squinching his lashy eyes and fixing them right on me, that you are willing to libel someone. And to that I said, Bishopric or not, I have been instructed by the Lord to give up my housecleaning and return to the Church—to the Light of the World Holiness Church to be exact. The Lord and I are going to air out that church. You libel that.

Canaan Johnson became suddenly very crooked-looking and said with his oily mouth, Well Mrs. Airwick we'll see how far you'll go. Savata sat sparkling in her coat and said nothing. I rose and with the air of a Bishop removed myself from that house.

Before Savata my fair sister and Canaan Johnson knew it, they had themselves a lawsuit on their hands. I sued for the Bishopric and for everything that went with it, the house in Brooklyn complete with rugs and slip covers, the lamb's wool coat and the diamond cluster. As they were purchased with the Light of the World Holiness Church's funds, they belonged to it, was my plea. The congregation, one big choir that called "Bishop Savata!" like a bunch of birds on a fence, was seated in the courthouse at the proceedings, and they did not take more than one half hour to outdo me. Although I sat on the stand barefooted and all my God's darkness vested in a Bishop's robe and preached an exposé against possessions in the Lord's name that rocked that courthouse—I said that the Lord don't have no checking account, owns no precious stones, displays nothing but a heart of gold and the natural hair of his head which was like the wool of the lamb, just as nature made it—it fell upon deaf ears. I said that the Prince of Darkness had come to roost on the steeple of the L.O.W.H.C. But do you think one bit that they cared? They hurrayed Canaan Johnson. They didn't any longer know a good sermon from a bad, Savata and her business manager had corroded them to see only the beauty that perisheth, not the God's lasting truth. They hurrayed Savata and hurrayed Canaan Johnson like some King and Queen. Naturally they won, the court handed down a verdict in their favor. I even had to pay the lawsuit expenses. Well, I went on ahousecleaning, as you know.

Time passed, and you can guess what came to pass . . . just what anybody in their right mind would expect. It only takes time. Mr. Canaan Johnson took his leave one day, without one note or how-do-you-do. Savata sent for me and I found her in tears and a nervous pout. My first question was what did he get, where is the coat and where is the cluster of diamonds? Savata thanked God that she had locked the lamb's wool coat in her cedar-lined closet to keep the moths out of it. But Canaan Johnson got away with the diamonds, naturally. Never mind, I smoothed her, let the Devil take the Devil's own; you got the coat out of it. But when we went to her cedar-lined closet and unlocked it what did we find but a regular moth picnic, they had made a feast of the coat. What they left wasn't enough lamb's wool to cover a baldheaded man. I could have said hoard thou not up treasures on earth but I kept my tongue, thank you Jesus.

Savata had her nervous breakdown and gave two full weeks to it. After it was over, she was meek as a lamb. We deeded the house in Brooklyn over to the old folks of the Light of the World Holiness Church and it was called the House of the Saints. But the church membership fell off to a handful of the faithful. Most wouldn't stay after Canaan and Savata were gone. They went on off and formed them a glamour church of their own. I got out my preaching papers and took over, preparing to build that church up again, this time on solid ground.

Oh I could have made Savata my fair sister eat crow and plenty of it, but I kept God's mercy and suggested with charity, as becomes a Bishop, that Savata take over my housecleaning jobs for a while until she could get herself straight. That could be her penance.

And that's why I've come by here to speak to you, to tell you that Savata my fair sister will be replacing me every Thursday from now on. I figure while she's on her knees in her repentance she might as well bend over and move around a little with a mopping rag in her hand; and while she's walking the floor astudying her sins, it will do her no harm to push along a vacuum cleaner ahead of herself. Her repentance, joined to practical uses, will therefore earn back a little of what her wickedness lost. In that way, sin can pay a little—and it will show Savata how little: $1.10 an hour, to be exact.

So thank you for listening to my story that has introduced you to Savata, my fair sister and your new cleaning woman. And thank you Jesus.

The Faces of Blood Kindred

James came to stay in his cousin's house when his mother was taken to the hospital with arthritis. The boys were both fourteen. James was blond and faintly harelipped, and he stuttered. His cousin was brown and shy. They had not much in common beyond their mysterious cousinhood, a bond of nature which they instinctively respected; though James mocked his cousin's habits, complained that he worried too much about things and was afraid of adventure. James owned and loved a flock of bantams, fought the cocks secretly, and his pockets jingled with tin cockspurs. His hands even had pecked places on them from fighting cocks in Mexican town.

James' father had run away to St. Louis some

years ago, and his mother Macel had gone to work as a seamstress in a dress factory in the city of Houston. Macel was blond and gay and good-natured, though the cousin's mother told his father that she had the Ganchion spitfire in her and had run her husband away and now was suffering for it with arthritis. When they went to the hospital to see Aunt Macel, the cousin looked at her hands drawn like pale claws against her breast and her stiffened legs braced down in splints. The cousin, white with commiseration, stood against the wall and gazed at her and saw her being tortured for abusing his uncle and driving him away from home and from his cousin James. James, when taken along by force, would stand at his mother's bedside and stare at her with a look of careless resignation. When she asked him questions he stammered incoherent answers.

James was this mysterious, wandering boy. He loved the woods at the edge of his cousin's neighborhood and would spend whole days there while his aunt called and searched for him by telephone. She would call the grandmother's house, talk to a number of little grandchildren who passed the phone from one to another and finally to the deaf old grandmother who could scarcely understand a word. But James was not there and no one had seen him. Once Fay, one of the young aunts living in the grandmother's house, called at midnight to say they had just discovered James sleeping under the fig trees in the back yard. Jock her husband had almost shot him before he had called out his name. Years later, when the cousin was in high school, he heard talk between his mother and father about Fay's hiding in the very same place while the police looked for her in the house—why, he did not know. At any rate, they had not found her.

He was a wild country boy brought to live in the city of Houston when his parents moved there from a little town down the road south. He said he wanted to be a cowboy, but it was too late for that; still, he wore boots and spurs. He hated the city, the schools, played away almost daily. The cousin admired James, thought him a daring hero. When he listened to his mother and father quarrel over James at night after they had gone to bed, his tenderness for him grew and grew. "He's like all the rest of them," his mother accused his father.

"They are my folks," the cousin's father said with dignity. "Macel is my sister."

"Then let some of the other folks take care of James. Let Fay. I simply cannot handle him."

Poor James, the cousin thought, poor homeless James. He has no friend but me.

One afternoon James suggested they go to see

some Cornish fighting cocks on a farm at the edge of the city. The cousin did not tell his mother and they stole away against his conscience. They hitchhiked to the farm out on the highway to Conroe, and there was a rooster-like man sitting barefooted in a little shotgun house. He had rooster feet, thin and with spread-out toes, and feathery hair. His wife was fat and loose and was barefooted, too. She objected to the cousin being there and said, "Chuck, you'll get yourself in trouble." But Chuck asked the cousins to come out to his chicken yard to see his Cornish cocks.

In a pen were the brilliant birds, each in its own coop, some with white scars about their jewel eyes. Stretching out beyond the chicken pen was the flat, rainy marshland of South Texas over which a web of gray mist hung. The sad feeling of after-rain engulfed the cousin and, mixed with the sense of evil because of the fighting cocks and his guilt at having left home secretly, made him feel speechless and afraid. He would not go in the pen but stood outside and watched James and Chuck spar with the cocks and heard Chuck speak of their prowess. Then the cousin heard James ask the price of a big blue cock with stars on its breast. "Fifteen dollars," Chuck said, "and worth a lots more. He fights like a fiend." To the cousin's astonishment he heard James say he would take the blue one, and he saw him take some bills from his pocket and separate fifteen single ones. When they left they heard Chuck and his wife quarreling in the little house.

They went on away to the highway to thumb a ride, and James tucked the blue cock inside his lumberjacket and spoke very quietly to him with his stuttering lips against the cock's blinking and magnificent ruby eye.

"But where will we keep him?" the cousin asked. "We can't at my house."

"I know a place," James said. "This Cornish will make a lot of money."

"But I'm afraid," the cousin said.

"You're always 'f-f-fraid," James said with a tender, mocking smile. And then he whispered something else to the black tip that stuck out from his jacket like a spur of ebony.

A pickup truck stopped for them shortly and took them straight to the Houston Heights where James said they would get out. James said they were going to their grandmother's house.

Their grandmother and grandfather had moved to the city, into a big rotten house, from the railroad town of Palestine, Texas. They had brought a family of seven grown children and the married children's children. In time, the grandfather had vanished and no one seemed to care where. The house was like a big boarding house, people in every room, the grandmother rocking, deaf and humped and shriveled, in the dining room. There was the smell of mustiness all through the house, exactly the way the grandmother smelled. In the back yard were some fig trees dripping with purple figs, and under the trees was a secret place, a damp and musky cove. It was a hideaway known to the children of the house, to the blackbirds after the figs, and to the cats stalking the birds. James told his cousin that this was the place to hide with the Cornish cock. He told the cock that he would have to be quiet for one night and made a chucking sound to him.

The cousins arrived at the grandmother's house with its sagging wooden front porch and its curtainless windows where some of the shades were pulled down. The front door was always open and the screen door sagged half-open. In the dirt front yard, which was damp and where cans and papers were strewn, two of the grandchildren sat quietly together: they were Jack and Little Sister whose mother was divorced and living there with her mother. They seemed special to the cousin because they were Catholics and had that strangeness about them. Their father had insisted that they be brought up in his church, though he had run away and left them in it long ago; and now they seemed to the cousin to have been abandoned in it and could never change back. No one would take them to Mass, and if a priest appeared on the sidewalk, someone in the house would rush out and snatch at the children or gather them away and shout at the priest to mind his own business and go away, as if he were a kidnapper.

"Our mother is sick in bed," Jack said to James and the cousin as they passed him and Little Sister in the yard. Their mother, Beatrice, was a delicate and wild woman who could not find her way with men, and later, when the cousin was in college, she took her life. Not long after, Little Sister was killed in an automobile crash—it was said she was running away to Baton Rouge, Louisiana, to get married to a Catholic gambler. But Jack went on his way somewhere in the world, and the cousin never saw him again. Years later he heard that Jack had gone to a Trappist Monastery away in the North, but no one knew for sure. James grumbled at Jack and Little Sister and whispered, "If-f-f you tell anybody we were here, then a bear will come tonight and e-e-*eat* you up in bed." The two little alien Catholics, alone in a churchless house, looked sadly and silently at James and the cousin. They were constantly together and the cousin thought how they protected each other, asked for nothing in their orphan's world; they were not afraid. "My pore little Cathlicks," the grandmother would sometimes say over them when she saw them sleeping together on the sleeping-porch, as if they were cursed.

James and the cousin went around the house and into the back yard. Now it was almost dark. They crept stealthily, James with the Cornish cock nestled under his lumberjack. Once it cawed. Then James hushed it by stroking its neck and whispering to it.

Under the fig trees, in the cloying sweetness of the ripe fruit, James uncovered the Cornish cock. He pulled a fig and ate a bite of it, then gave a taste of it to the cock who snapped it fiercely. Before the cousins knew it he had leapt to the ground and, as if he were on springs, bounced up into a fig tree. The Cornish cock began at once to eat the figs. Jim murmured an oath and shook the tree. Figs fat and wet fell upon him and the cousin.

"Stop!" the cousin whispered. "You'll ruin Granny's figs."

"Shut up." James scowled. "You're always 'f-f-fraid."

The cousin picked up a rock from the ground and threw it into the tree. He must have hurled it with great force, greater than he knew he possessed, for in a flash there shuddered at his feet the dark leafy bunch of the Cornish cock. In a moment the feathers were still.

"I didn't mean to, I didn't mean to!" the cousin gasped in horror, and he backed farther and farther away, beyond the deep shadows of the fig trees. Standing away, he saw in the dark luscious grove the figure of James fall to the ground and kneel over his Cornish cock and clasp the tousled mass like a lover's head. He heard him sob softly; and the cousin backed away in anguish.

As he passed the curtainless windows of the dining room where the light was now on, he saw his old grandmother hunched in her chair, one leg folded under her, rocking gently and staring at nothing; and she seemed to him at that moment to be bearing the sorrow of everything—in her house, under the fig trees, in all the world. And then he heard the soft cries of Beatrice from her mysterious room, "Somebody help me, somebody go bring me a drink of water." He went on, past the chaos of the sleeping-porch that had so many beds and cots in it—for Beatrice's two children the little Catholics, for Fay's two, for his grandmother, for his grandfather who would not stay home, for Fay and for Jock the young seaman, her third husband, with tattoos and still wearing his sailor pants. He thought of Jock who cursed before everybody, was restless, would come and go or sprawl on the bed he and Fay slept in on the sleeping porch with all the rest; and he remembered when he had stayed overnight in this house once how he had heard what he thought was Jock beating Fay in the night, crying out to her and panting, "you f . . ."; how Jock the sailor would lie on the bed in the daytime smoking and reading from a storage of battered *Western Stories* and *Romance Stories* magazines that were strewn under the bed, while Fay worked at the Palais Royale in town selling ladies' ready-to-wear, and the voice of Beatrice suddenly calling overall, "Somebody! Please help me, I am so sick." Once the cousin had gone into her sad room when no one else would and she had pled, startled to see him there, and with a stark gray face scarred by the delicate white cleft of her lip, "Please help your Aunt Bea get a little ease from this headache; reach under the mattress—don't tell anybody —your Aunt Bea has to have some rest from this pain—reach right yonder under the mattress and give her that little bottle. That's it. This is our secret, and you mustn't ever tell a soul." Within five years she was to die, and why should this beautiful Beatrice have to lie in a rest home, alone and none of her family ever coming to see her, until the home sent a message that she was dead? But he thought, hearing of her death, that if he had secretly helped ease her suffering, he had that to know, without ever telling—

until he heard them say that she had died from taking too many pills from a hidden bottle.

The cousin walked away from the grandmother's house and went the long way home under the fresh evening sky, his fingers sticky with fig musk, leaving James and the dead cock under the fig trees. If he could one day save all his kindred from pain or help them to some hope! "I will, I will!" he promised. But what were they paying penance for? What was their wrong? Later he knew it bore the ancient name of lust. And as he walked on he saw, like a sparkling stone hurling toward him over the Natural Gas Reservoir, the first star break the heavens—who cast it?—and he wished he might die by it. When he approached the back door of his house, there was the benevolent figure of his mother in the kitchen fixing supper and he wondered how he would be able to tell her and his father where he had been and what had happened to James. "We went to the woods," he cried, "and James ran away." Later that night when James did not come back, his father telephoned the grandmother's house. But no one there had seen him.

The cousin cried himself to sleep that night, lonely and guilty, grieving for much more than he knew, but believing, in that faithful way of children, that in time he might know what it all meant, and that it was a matter of waiting, confused and watchful, until it came clear, as so much of everything promised to, in long time; and he dreamt of a blue rooster with stars on its breast sitting in a tree of bitter figs, crowing a doom of suffering over the house of his kinfolks.

James stayed away for three days and nights; and on the third night they had a long-distance call from James' father in St. Louis, saying that James had come there dirty and tired and stuttering. They had not seen each other for seven years.

Long later the cousin was in a large Midwestern city where some honor was being shown him. Suddenly in the crowded hall a face emerged from the gathering of strangers and moved toward him. It seemed the image of all his blood kin: was it that shadow-face that tracked and haunted him? It was James' face, and at that glance there glimmered over it some dreamlike umbrageous distortion of those long-ago boy's features, as if the cousin saw that face through a pane of colored glass or through currents of time that had deepened over it as it had sunk into its inheritance.

There was something James had to say, it was on his face; but what it was the cousin never knew, for someone pulled him round, his back to James, to shake his hand and congratulate him—someone of distinction. When he finally turned, heavy as stone, as if he were turning to look back into the face of his own secret sorrow, James was gone; and the cousins never met again.

But the look upon James' face that moment that night in a strange city where the cousin had come to passing recognition and had found a transient homage, bore the haunting question of ancestry; and though he thought he had at last found and cleared for himself something of identity, a particle of answer in the face of the world, had he set anything at peace, answered any speechless question, atoned for the blind failing, the outrage and the pain on the face of his blood kindred? That glance, struck like a blow against ancestral countenance, had left a scar of resemblance, ancient and unchanging through the generations, on the faces of the grandmother, of the aunts, the cousins, his own father and his father's father; and would mark his own face longer than the stamp of any stranger's honor that would change nothing.

Old Wildwood

On a soft morning in May, at the American Express in Rome, the grandson was handed a letter; and high up on the Spanish Steps he sat alone and opened the letter and read its news. It was in his mother's hand:

"Well, your grandaddy died two days ago and we had his funeral in the house in Charity. There were so many flowers, roses and gladiolas and every other kind, that the front porch was filled with them, twas a sight to see. Then we took him to the graveyard where all the rest are buried and added his grave, one more, to the rest.

"At the graveyard your father suddenly walked out and stood and said the Lord's Prayer over his daddy's grave, as none of the Methodists in the family would hear a Catholic priest say a Catholic prayer, nor the Catholics in the family allow a Methodist one; and your grandaddy was going to be left in his grave without one holy word of any kind. But both were there, priest and preacher, and I said what a shame that your poor old daddy has to go to earth without even 'Abide with Me' sung by a soloist. His own begotten children marrying without conscience into this church and that, confounding their children as to the nature of God, caused it all, and there it was to see, clear and shameful, at the graveyard. Then all of a sudden your two great aunts, my mother's and your grandmother's sweet old sisters, Ruby and Saxon Thompson, one blind and the other of such strutted ankles from Bright's Disease as could barely toddle, started singing 'Just As I Am Without One Plea,' and many joined in, it was so sweet and so sad and so peaceful to hear. Then we all walked away and left your grandaddy in his grave."

The grandson lifted his eyes from the letter and they saw an ancient foreign city of stone. So an old lost grandfather, an old man of timber, had left the world. He folded the letter and put it in his pocket. Then he leaned back and settled upon the pocked stone of the worn steps, supporting himself upon the opened palm of his hand. He rested a little, holding the letter, thinking how clear pictures of what had troubled his mind always came to him in some sudden, quiet ease of resting. He considered, as a man resting on stone, his grandfather.

Yes, he thought, the little old grandfather had the animal grace and solitary air of an old mariner about him, though he was a lumberman and purely of earth. His left leg was shorter than his right, and the left foot had some flaw in it that caused the shoe on it to curl upwards. The last time the grandson had seen his grandfather was the summer day when, home on leave from the Navy, and twenty-one, he had come out into the back yard in his shining officer's uniform to find his grandfather sitting there snowy-headed and holding his cap in his hand. Grandfather and grandson had embraced and the grandfather had wept. How so few years had changed him, the grandson had thought that afternoon: so little time had whitened his head and brought him to quick tears: and the grandson heard in his head the words of a long time back, spoken to him by his grandfather that night in Galveston, "Go over into Missi'ppi one day and see can you find your kinfolks . . ."

Where had the grandfather come from, that summer afternoon? Where had he been all these years? The grandson had scarcely thought of him. And now, suddenly, on that summer day of leave, he had heard his mother call to his father, "Your *daddy's* here," with an intonation of shame; and then his mother had come into his room and said, "Son, your grandaddy's here. Go out in the back yard and see your grandaddy."

When he had put on his uniform and stepped into

the yard, there he saw the white-headed little man sitting on the bench. And there, resting on the grass and lying a little on its side as though it were a separate being, curled and dwarfed, was his grandfather's crooked foot, old disastrous companion.

The grandfather was an idler and had been run away from home, it was said, by his wife and children time and time again, and the last time for good; and where did he live and what did he do? Later, on the day of his visit and after he had gone away, the grandson's mother had confessed that she knew her husband went secretly to see his father somewhere in the city and to give him money the family had to do without. It was in a shabby little hotel on a street of houses of women and saloons that his father and his grandfather met and talked, father and son.

As he sat with his grandfather in the yard on the white bench under the camphor tree that summer, and now on this alien stone, the grandson remembered that the first time he had known his grandfather was on the trip to Galveston where they went to fish—the grandson was fourteen—and how lonesome he was there with this little old graying limping stranger who was his grandfather and who was wild somewhere that the grandson could not surmise, only fear. Who was this man tied to him by blood through his father and who, though he strongly resembled his father, seemed an alien, not even a friend. The grandfather had sat on the rocks and drunk whiskey while the grandson fished; and though he did not talk much, the grandson felt that there was a constant toil of figuring going on in the old man as he looked out over the brown Gulf water, his feet bare and his shoes on the rock, one crooked one by one good one. On the rock the boy gazed at the bad foot for a long, long time, more often than he watched the fishing line, as though the foot on the rock might be some odd creature he had brought up from the water and left on the rock to perish in the sun. At night he watched it too, curled on the cot in the moonlight as his grandfather slept, so that he came to know it well on both rock and cot and to think of it as a special kind of being in itself. There on the rock, as on the cot, the bad foot was the very naked shape of the shoe that concealed it. It seemed lifeless there on the rock, it was turned inwards toward the good foot as though to ask for pity from it or to caricature it. The good foot seemed proud and aloof and disdainful, virile and perfectly shaped.

On the rock, the grandfather was like a man of the sea, the grandson thought, like a fisherman or a boat captain. His large Roman head with its bulging forehead characteristic of his children shone in the sun; and his wide face was too large for his small and rather delicate body, lending him a strangely noble bearing, classic and Bacchian. There was something deeply kind and tender in this old gentleman grandfather barefooted on the rock, drinking whiskey from the bottle. The grandson felt the man was often at the point of speaking to him of some serious thing but drank it all away again out of timidity or respect.

Each night they straggled back to their room in a cheap Gulf-front cabin full of flies and sand, and the grandson would help his grandfather into his cot where he would immediately fall to sleep. Then the grandson would lie for a long time watching his grandfather breathe, his graying curly hair tousled over his strutted forehead, and watching the sad foot that sometimes flinched on the sheet with fatigue, for it was a weak foot, he thought. Considering this man before him, the grandson thought how he might be a man of wood, grown in a wilderness of trees, as rude and native and unblazed as a wildwood tree. He held some wilderness in him, the very sap and seed of it. Then, half fearing the man, the grandson would fall asleep, with the thought and the image of the blighted foot worrying him. He was always afraid of his grandfather, no doubt because of the whiskey, but certainly for deeper, more mysterious reasons which he could not find out in this man who was yet so respectful to him.

One night after the grandfather had been drinking on the rock all day, he had drunk some more in the cabin and finally, sitting on the side of his cot, he had found the words he had to say to the grandson. He had spoken to him clearly and quietly and in such a kind of flowing song that the words might have been given him by another voice whispering him what to say.

"We all lived in Missi'ppi," was the way he began, quietly, to speak. "And in those days wasn't much there, only sawmills and wildwoods of good rich timber, uncut and unmarked, and lots of good Nigras to help with everything, wide airy houses and broad fields. It all seems now such a good day and time, though we didn't count it for much then. Your granny and I moved over out of Missi'ppi and into Texas, from one little mill town to another, me blazing timber and then cutting it, counting it in the railroad cars, your granny taking a new baby each time, seems like, but the same baby buggy for each—if we'd have named our children after the counties they were borned in, all twelve of them, counting the one that died in Conroe, you'd have a muster roll of half the counties of Texas—all borned in Texas; but not a one ever went back to Missi'ppi, nor cared. Twas all wildwood then, son, but so soon gone.

"I had such man's strength then, the kind that first my grandfather broke wilderness with into trail and clearing, hewed houses and towns out of timber with, the kind his grandsons used to break the rest. Why I fathered twelve children in the state of Texas and fed them on sweet milk and kidney beans and light bread and working twelve hours a day—mill and railroad—working Nigras and working myself and raising a family of barefooted towheads chasing the chickens and climbing the trees and carrying water, playing tree tag in the dirt yard stained with mulberries. Your granny wasn't deaf then, had better hearing than most, could hear the boll weevils in the cotton, could listen that well. We all slept all over the house, beds never made, always a baby squalling in the kitchen while your granny cooked, or eating dirt where it sat in the shade as your granny did the washing in the washpot on the fire with Nigras helping and singing, or riding the hip of one of the big girls or boys . . . my children grew up on each other's hips and you could never tell it now the way they live and treat each other.

"I didn't have any schooling, but my grandfather was a schoolteacher and broke clearing and built a log schoolhouse and taught in it—it still stands, I hear tell, in Tupolo—and lived to start a university in Stockton, Missi'ppi; was a Peabody and the Peabodys still live all over Missi'ppi, go in there and you'll find Peabodys all over Missi'ppi. You know there's a big bridge of steel over the Missi'ppi River at Meridian; that's a Peabody, kin to me and kin to you. Another one, John Bell, built a highway clean to the Louisiana line and starting at Jackson; that's some of your kinfolks, old John Bell, such a fine singing man, a good voice and pure black-headed Irishman with his temper in his eyes. Called him Cousin Jack, he was adopted, and just here in Galveston, to tell you the truth, I've been wondering again who from; I've wondered often about John Bell all these years, studied him time and again. When I came he was already in our family, running with the other children in the yard, seems like, when I first saw him, and we all called him Cousin Jack, and of all my family, brother and sister and even my own children, John Bell was the best friend ever in this world to me. Aw, John Bell's been heavy on my mind—John Bell! He was one to go to. Cousin Jack was not ascared of anything, brave everywhere he went and not ascared of hard work, spit on his hands and went right in. Went to work at fourteen and helped the family. Was a jolly man and full of some of the devil, too, and we raised a ruckus on Saturday nights when we was young men together, we'd dance till midnight, court the girls on the way home and come on home ourselves singing and in great spirits. John Bell! Fishing and singing on the river with a pint of bourbon in our hip pocket and a breath of it on the bait for good luck. But something always a little sad about John Bell, have never known what it could be. Maybe it was his being adopted. He knew that; they told him. But it was more than that. Then he married Nellie Clayton, your Granny's niece, and I have never seen him again. He built a highway clean through the state of Missi'ppi and I always knew he would amount to something. Died in 1921, and now his children are all up and grown in Missi'ppi. They are some of the ones to look for. Find the Bells.

"Time came when all the tree country of East Texas was cut, seemed like no timber left, and new ways and new mills. I brought all my family to Houston, to work for the Southern Pacific. Some was married and even had babies of their own, but we stayed together, the whole kit and kaboodle of us, all around your granny. In the city of Houston we found one big old house and all lived in it. Then the family began to sunder apart, seemed like, with some going away to marry and then coming home again bringing husband or wife. I stayed away from home as much as I could, to have some peace from all the clamoring among my children. I never understood my children, son, could never make them out, my own children; children coming in and going out, half their children living there with this new husband and that, and the old husbands coming back to make a fuss, and one, Grace's, just staying on there, moved in and wouldn't ever leave, is still there to this day; and children from all husbands and wives playing all together in that house, with your granny deaf as a doornail and calling out to the children to mind, and wanting care, but would never leave and never will, she'll die in that house with all of them around her, abusing her, too, neither child nor grandchild minding her. I just left, son, and went to live in a boarding house. I'd go home on Sundays and on Easters and on Christmas, but not to stay. There's a time when a person can't help anything any more, anything. Still, they would come to me, one or another of my sons and daughters, but not to see how I was or to bring me anything, twas to borrow money from me. They never knew that I had lost my job with the S.P. because I drank a little whiskey.

"And I never went to any church, son, but I'm fifty years of age and I believe in the living God and practice the Golden Rule and I hope the Lord'll save me from my sins. But I never had anybody to go to, for help or comfort, and I want you to know your father didn't either, never had anybody to go to. But I want you to know you do, and I will tell you who and where so you will always know. I don't want you ever to know what it is not to have anybody to go to.

"So when you get to be a young man I hope you'll go over into Missi'ppi and see can you find your blood kinfolks. Tell them your grandaddy sent you there. Haven't been over there myself for thirty years, kept meaning to but just never did. Now I guess I never will. But you go, and when you go, tell them you are a Peabody's grandson. They're all there, all over there, all over Missi'ppi; look for the Peabodys and for the Claytons and look for the Bells . . ."

After the grandfather had finished his story, he sat still on his cot, looking down as if he might be regarding his bare crooked foot. The grandson did not speak or ask a question but he lay quietly thinking about it all, how melancholy and grand the history of relations was. Then, in a while, he heard his grandfather get up softly, put on his crooked shoe and the good one, and go out, thinking he was asleep. He has gone to find him John Bell, the grandson thought. The creaking of his bad shoe and the rhythm of his limp seemed to the grandson to repeat his grandfather's words: Peabodys and the Claytons and the Bells.

The grandson did not sleep while his grandfather was gone. He was afraid, for the tides of the Gulf were swelling against the sea wall below the cabin; yet he thought how he no longer feared his grandfather, for now that he had spoken to him so quietly and with such love he felt he was something of his own. He loved his grandfather. Yet now that he had been brought to love what he had feared, he was cruelly left alone in the whole world with this love, it seemed, and was that the way love worked?—with the unknown waters swelling and falling close to the bed where he lay with the loving story haunting him? There was so much more to it all, to the life of men and women, than he had known before he came to Galveston just to fish with his grandfather, so much in just a man barefooted on a rock and drinking whiskey in the sun, silent and dangerous and kin to him. And then the man had spoken and made a bond between them and brought a kind of nobility of forest, something like a shelter of grandness of trees over it all. The tree country! The grandson belonged to an old, illustrious bunch of people of timber with names he could now name, all a busy, honorable and worthy company of wilderness breakers and forest blazers, bridge builders and road makers, and teachers, Claytons and Peabodys and Bells, and the grandfather belonged to them, too, and it was he who had brought all the others home to him, his grandson. Yet the grandfather seemed an orphan. And now for the first time, the grandson felt the deep, free sadness of orphanage; and he knew he was orphaned, too. That was the cruel gift of his grandfather, he thought. The crooked foot! John Bell!

In this loneliness he knew, at some border where land turned into endless water, he felt himself to be the only one alive in this moment—where were all the rest?—in a land called Mississippi, called Texas, where? He was alone to do what he could do with it all and oh what to do would be some daring thing, told or performed on some shore where two ancient elements met, land and water, and touched each other and caused some violence of kinship between two orphans, and with heartbreak in it. What to do would have the quiet, promising dangerousness of his grandfather on the rock in it, it would have the grave and epic tone of his grandfather's ultimate telling on the side of the cot under one light globe in a mist of shoreflies in a sandy transient roof of revelation while the tide washed at the very feet of teller and listener. And what to do would have the feeling of myth and mystery that he felt as he had listened, as though when he listened he were a rock and the story he heard was water swelling and washing over generations and falling again, like the waters over the rock when the tide came in.

Suddenly he heard footsteps, and when the door opened quietly he saw his grandfather and a woman behind him. They came in the room and the woman whispered, "You didn't tell me that a kid was here."

"He's asleep, John Bell," the grandfather whispered.

Something began between the two, between the grandfather and the woman, and the grandson feigned sleep. But he watched through the lashes of his half-closed eyes as through an ambush of grass the odd grace of his grandfather struggling with the woman with whom he seemed to be swimming through water, and he heard his grandfather's low growl like a fierce dog on the cot, and he saw his grandfather's devil's foot treading and gently kicking, bare in the air, so close to him that he could have reached out to touch it. And then he knew that the foot had a very special beauty and grace of moment, a lovely secret performance hidden in it that had seemed a shame on his person and a flaw upon the rock. It had something, even, of a bird's movements in it. It was the crooked foot that was the source and the meaning of the strange and lovely and somehow delicate disaster on the bed; and it was that shape and movement that the grandson took for his own to remember.

John Bell!

The two people drank out of a bottle without saying a word, but they were celebrating something they had come through, as if they had succeeded in swimming, with each other's help, a laborious dangerous distance; and then they rose to leave the room together. But at the door, the grandfather called softly as he lifted the bottle once more to his mouth, "For John Bell . . . ," and the name rang deeply over the dark room like the tone of a bell upon the sea.

When they were gone, the grandson rose and looked out the window and saw the water with a horned moon over it and smelled the limey odors of shrimp, saw the delicate swaying starry lights of fishing boats; and there in the clear light of the moon he saw the rock he and his grandfather fished on. The tide was climbing over it and slipping back off it as if to cover it with a sighing embrace, like a body, as if to pull the rock, for a swelling moment, to its soft and caressing bosom of water; and there was a secret bathing of tenderness over the very world like a dark rock washed over with moonlit sea water and whiskey and tenderness and the mysteriousness of a grandfather, of an old story, an old ancestor of whom the grandson was afraid again. Now the grandfather seemed to the grandson to have been some old sea-being risen out of the waters to sit on a rock and to tell a tale in a stranger's room, and disappear. Would he ever come again to fish on the rock in the Gulf and to snore on the cot in the cabin? But as he looked at the world of rock and tide and moon, in the grandson's head the words of a pioneer sounded, quiet and plaintive and urgent: Go over into Missi'ppi when you get to be a young man and see can you find your kinfolks, son. Look for the Claytons and look for the Peabodys and look for the Bells, all in there, all over Missi'ppi . . . And the bell-rung deepness of a name called sounded in the dark room.

John Bell!

There in the room, even then, alone and with the wild lovely world he knew, tidewater and moonlight tenderly tormenting the rock outside, and inside the astonishing delicate performance tormenting the room, and the shape of the foot on both room and rock, the grandson thought how he would do, in his time, some work to bring about through an enduring rock-silence a secret performance with something, some rock-force, some tide-force, some lovely, hearty, fine wildwood wildwater thing always living in him through his ancestry and now brought to sense in him, that old gamy wilderness bequeathed him; how shaggy-headed, crooked-footed perfection would be what he would work for, some marvelous, reckless and imperfect loveliness, proclaiming about the ways of men in the world and all that befell them, all that glorified, all that damned them, clearing and covering over and clearing again, on and on and on.

He went back to his cot and lay upon his young back. Not to go to sleep! but to stay awake with it all, whatever, whatever it was, keeping the wilderness awake in this and many more rooms, breathing seawind and pinesap. Because—now he felt sure—the thing to do about it all and with it all would be in some performance of the senses after long silence and waiting—of the hair that would grow upon his chest like grass and of the nipples of his breast, of the wildwood in his seed and the sappy sweat of the crease of his loins, of the saltwater of his tears, the spit on his palms, the blistering of the blazer's ax-handle, all mortal stuff. To keep wilderness awake and wild and never sleeping, in many rooms in many places was his plan in Galveston, and the torment that lay ahead for him would come, and it would hold him wakeful through nights of bitter desire for more than he could ever name, but for some gentle, lovely and disastrous heartbreak of men and women in this world. And in that room that held the history of his grandfather, the little poem of his forebears and the gesture of the now beautiful swimming and soaring crooked foot, he knew for himself that there would be, or he would make them, secret rooms in his life holding, like a gymnasium, the odors of mortal exertion, of desperate tournament, a violent contest, a hardy, laborious chopping, manual and physical and involving the strength in his blistering hands and the muscles of his heaving back, all the blazer's work, the pioneer's blazing hand! Or places upon rocks of silence where an enigma lay in the sun, dry and orphaned and moribund until some blessed tide eventually rose and caressed it and took it to its breast as if to whisper, "Belong to me before I slide away," and what was silent and half-dead roused and showed its secret performance: that seemed to be the whole history of everything, the secret, possible performance in everything that was sliding, sliding away.

Finally, his breast aching and its secret that lived there unperformed, but with the trembling of some enormous coming thrill, the distant disclosure of some vision, even, of some glimmering company of humanity of his yearning with whom to perform some daring, lovely, heartbroken and disastrous history; and with terror of listener and sadness of teller, the grandson fell alone to sleep and never heard his grandfather come back to his cot, that night in Galveston.

Now they had buried the grandfather. Bury the good man of wilderness, he thought; bury in Texas dirt the crooked foot that never walked again on the ground of Missi'ppi where mine has never been set. And find him John Bell in the next world.

His hand upon which he had rested was aching and he relieved it of his weight and sat upon the solid slab of ancient Travertine stone. There, engraved in the palm of the hand he had leaned on, was the very mark and grain of the stone, as though his hand were stone. He would not have a hand of stone! He would carry a hand that could labor wood and build a house, trouble dirt and lay a highway, and blaze a trail through leaf and bramble; and a hand that could rot like wood and fall into dust.

And then the grandson thought how all the style and works of stone had so deeply troubled him in this ancient city, and how he had not clearly known until now that he loved wood best and belonged by his very secret woodsman's nature to old wildwood.

The Moss Rose

"Portulaca," the Third Avenue man said to him at the door of his shop when he asked the name of what he thought was a box of moss-rose plants for sale on the sidewalk.

"Aren't they moss roses?" he asked.

"Portulaca," the man said.

"Do they have orange and yellow and crimson blossoms?"

"That's right," the man said.

"And they aren't moss roses?"

"Portulaca," he said again.

He went on up Third Avenue saying the word to himself as he walked, so as not to forget it. *Portulaca.* "I guess that's what they call them up here," he said to himself.

He had grown up with them—*moss roses*—always in some flower bed, by a grave, by a pump where the ground was moist, in a hanging kettle on a porch. They were a part of another landscape, a flower il-

memory. But it has caused something: a change, an attitude, an aspect. It is the effect of what was, he thought, going on, that is the long-lastingness in us.

Thinking this, he looked up at the sides of the buildings and saw that the "Portulaca" grew here and there on the Third Avenue people's fire escapes. It was a rather common summer flower on Third Avenue! Well, the moss rose belongs to them, too, as it did to the old guard back home, he thought. Somehow the little moss rose was a part of any old order, any old, passing bunch, and it clung to those who represented the loss of old fixtures of everyday life, it was that faithful a friend. Now it seemed right that it grow along Third Avenue in boxes and pots on rusty and cluttered and bedraggled fire escapes, as it had in a house he knew once that was inhabited by a flock of raggle-taggle kinfolks, full of joy and knowing trouble and taggling and scrabbling along, a day at a time, toward a better day, surely, they avowed. So, in that old home far away, the moss rose used to look out on a train track, though the scarce train was an event when it chose to pass that way, as if it might be some curious animal out of the woods that had taken a daring path by the house. Still, something of the same configuration was here.

Portulaca! Little moss rose! he thought. The same patterns do exist all over the world, in cities and towns, wherever people live and arrange life around themselves, a bridge over a creek or a tunnel under a river, there is a way to manage. And a sudden sight of this human pattern in one place restores a lost recognition of it in another, far away, through an eternal image of a simple flower, in the hands and care of both; and in a moment's illumination there was in him the certain knowledge of unity forever working to stitch and tie, like a quilt, the human world into a simple shape of repetition and variation of what seems a meaningless and haphazard design whose whole was hostile to its parts and seemed set on disordering them.

He went back to the shop and told the man he would like to try a Portulaca plant. On his fire escape, just off Third Avenue, it would grow and bloom the fragile starlike blossoms of the moss rose he had loved so deeply in another place and would love here as well, though it might be a little different from the old one—something in the leaf, slight but different. Yet, everything changes, he thought, slowly it all changes. Do we resign ouselves to that? Is youth passing when we see this—the fierce battle of youth that would not accept change and loss? But there is always the relationship of sameness, too, in all things, which identifies the old ancestor: the *relatedness;* we'll cling to that, to that continuous stem around which only the adornments change, he thought. What if the leaf is a little different? The family is the same . . . the bloom is akin—Portulaca or moss rose. Though the El was gone and the house of kinfolk vanished, two beings as different as man and woman, he would water and tend and foster the old moss-rose family that was still going on.

Sitting on his fire escape, after planting the moss rose in a discarded roasting pan, he looked out through the grillwork of the fire escape and saw the gaunt white-headed man who resembled so much his grandfather in his small room across the courtyard through the Trees of Heaven, where he sat night and day, serene and waiting. Where was his home? Did he know a land where the moss rose bloomed? In his waiting, in his drab, monotonous loneliness, there was a memory living, surely. Who knew, one day it might freshen in him at the sight of something that lingered in the world out of his past, right in the neighborhood, just out of his window, and gladden him for an hour.

Squatting on the fire escape, he thought of his own dreams and hopes. As he sat with the little plant, gazing at it for a long time, a memory rose from it like a vapor, eluded him, and sank back into it. He sat patiently, to catch the memory that glimmered over the petals. What hummingbird remembrance, elusive and darting from his mind, still took its flavor, its bit of sweetness, from the moss rose? And then it came up clear and simple to him, the memory in the moss rose.

It was in the back yard of The Place, as it was called by all who lived there, long ago, under a cool shade tree in Texas. A clump of moss roses grew, without anybody asking it to, in the moist ground around the pump like ringlets of hair wreathed with red and orange and yellow blossoms. He had hung the bucket by its handle over the neck of the pump, and Jessy his small sister held one of his hands while he jacked the pump with the other. The chinaberry trees were still fresh before the sun would make them limp, the chickens were pert, the dew was still on everything, even the woodpile, and the sand in the road still cool. Their old Cherokee rose, that his grandmother had planted when she was a young woman in this house, was gay and blooming at every leaf and thorn, and frolicking all over the fence, down and up and around, locking itself and freeing itself—it would quieten down in the hot afternoon.

Over the squeaking of the pump, he heard a voice and a word . . . "star . . . star." He turned to Jessy and saw that she had picked one of the moss roses and offered it to him, a tiny red star, on the palm of her hand. The bloom was so wonderous and the gift so sudden that he had thought, at that moment, that all life might be something like this twinkling offering. When they went in, the bucket filled, and their mother asked what they had been doing, Jessy had answered, "Picking stars . . ."

Now the place was gone, the water dried up, no doubt, the moss rose finished. Jessy was dead these many years; moss roses grew around her small grave —unless they had been overcome by weeds; he had not gone back to that graveyard for a long time. Here on his fire escape (the landlady had once advertised it as a "renovated terrace") was a fragile remnant of that vanished world; he would tend it; it would no doubt bloom, in time. To find that simple joy again, what could he do to recapture it, to recapture what had been, long ago in the moss rose and in himself— that ready acceptance, that instantaneous belief, in that pure joy of morning, in one sweet summer, long ago at the water pump, holding his sister's tiny hand? All that had followed, as he had grown, dimmed and tarnished that small blinking star: error and disenchantment and loss.

I used to dream of a little fresh sunrise town like that one where we stood once, at the water pump, he said to himself, where I would be, as fixed upon the ground as the moss rose round the pump, rising in the early morning in vigor to my work and moving and living round it, drawing more and more life to it, through me. Instead, work and life seem to have withdrawn from me more and more, to have pushed life back from where it began, into cities and stone buildings, onto pavements, to have impoverished me even of memories that would save me despair, in a huge grassless city where no flowers bloom on the ground.

When the moss rose bloomed again for him, this time on a fire escape in a great city where he sat with gray streaks in his hair, he would be grateful for that. There might even grow another star to pick. So he would watch, day by day, for the flowers to appear, speaking patiently to himself, and again for the hundredth time, that some change was imperative round which to rebuild, out of which to call back the fullness of forgotten signs of love and visions of hope. Believe that it is right ahead, he said to himself, sitting with the plant on the fire escape. Start with one little plain, going-on thing to live around and to take up an old beginning from. Until slowly, slowly, hope and new life will grow and leaf out from it to many places and to many old forgotten promises.

The Armadillo Basket

Each spring the two sisters from Crockett would drive fifty miles to the little town of Charity for their annual work on the family plot in the Charity Cemetery. They would bring potted plants and ferns and seeds for old-maids and periwinkles. In the mornings they would ride from the old family house where their sister Laura lived—she had kept it all these years—to the graveyard at the edge of town. Then they would sit under the cypress trees around the big rectangle that held the generations: their father and mother Mary and William Starnes, the two Starnes grandparents, a memorial marker for their young brother, Son, killed in France in the world war and buried somewhere over there, and their baby sister who had died in the flu epidemic. Here they would talk about the early days when they were all in Charity, three generations living together in the wide family house, work in the dirt plot with spades and forks, and shape up the worn graves.

Laura would never go, said the dead were "gone somewhere else, now, and not in graves," and that their memory was alive in the house they had lived in. She was peculiar that way. She lived by superstitions and signs and omens. But Lucy and Mary knew that it was her feelings that kept her from the family graves; she could not bear it; Laura was the emotional one, holding to the past and still refusing to give it up. She kept it alive by living within it, in the old house where she moved about, day by day, as though all were still there. Lucy and Mary, modernized and flourishing somewhat in the growing town of progress, Crockett, Texas, and having fairly successful husbands, railroad men, chided Laura for her refusal to face the "reality of today"; but their reprovals had slowly weakened into an indulgence of her hidebound ways, which seemed to shame their change and was what they really wanted for themselves, and so they came to humor her. They felt, secretly, indeed, that Laura kept the world they had lost, she presided over it, saving it and protecting it within that house so that they could re-enter it every spring: there it was, as it had always been, waiting for them when they opened the front door with its frosted pane decorated with the fancy figure of a man riding a horse with frosty mane and flourishing frosty tail. The keeping of the graves, then, was *their* work, the honoring gesture toward what was gone, the tending of its dirt remains, though they would not admit it, even to themselves. They regarded it as a work of plain and practical duty, they declared. Laura, the spit image of her mother and the eldest of the family, living just as her mother had, as though she were continuing the life of her mother in this house, would not talk of it.

This morning they had started late, for Laura had suddenly said she would go with her sisters to the cemetery. She had started coiling up her hair into its knot on the back of her head, holding the hairpins in her mouth and saving the combed-out wisps of hair for the hair receiver on her dresser that still held the combings of her mother's hair and had been hers before. But an omen had happened on her dresser: her photograph of Mama, that had one eye eaten out by something in that cedar chest where it had been stored one winter, fell face down. Laura had got up from the dresser, in a kind of spell, and had gone back to the breezeway where Lucy and Mary were waiting, holding their breath, and said, "You all better go on, I've got some butterbeans to shell," and turned and walked back to her bedroom with a piece of her hair hanging down. "But why don't you pack shade. I hope you'll all keep me in the shade after I'm buried. It's awful to think of lying out under the glaring sun all day, or in the rain. And a cedar smells so good."

"Yes, it does."

"And I want a little something blooming all the time."

"I like little East Texas moss roses. Or maybe Shasta daisies in the summer."

"And a good big mound, kept all round and smooth. It would kill me to think my grave was flat or all run-down on one side like an old shoe. A person's folks should keep her grave looking nice as long as they have hands to do it."

Mary whined a little. They worked silently, shadowed by the certainty that they, too, would one day have a grave of their own to be kept.

"I remember when Mama used to bring us here. I remember the great big grasshoppers, how they'd fly like fat birds. The boys said they spat tobacco juice and that if it hit your eye, it'd put it out. And how they warned us not to drink out of the hydrants because the water was poisoned by the dead."

"I remember the old dried flowers scattered after a rain and their sick wet smell, like a morgue."

"And all the names and years on the stones."

"And the neat little graves of babies."

A sheath of silence slipped over the two, as close as a glove over the hand. They sat mute, remembering the dead little sister Mary Lou, a fragile little girl born into the epidemic when they were just young girls and died from it within the month.

"Well—the graves. We've a lot of work to do."

"Son . . ." Mary sadly called his name. "Remember the flag we hung in our window for him when he was over there? And how they burned Old Man Gloom in town by the Show, to keep up the spirit."

"Wonder what his life would have been like. He was just like Papa."

"I think it will rain. That would ruin everything."

They started throwing up fresh earth with their little spades. In the west, over a pack of little Negro shacks leaning against each other, a big mound of gray cloud was swelling and sliding up to the sun to obscure it. A muffled rumbling rolled through it like a faraway wagon over an old bridge.

Suddenly a weak, slack-faced little man stood out from a cypress tree and said, "Good day, ladies." It was Mr. Crocus.

"Oh, Mr. Crocus!" Lucy shouted and dropped her palmetto rake, a little frightened. "We are working again, you see."

"Yes, ma'am. It takes a lot of labor, you know,

women were closing the windows and the wind began to ruffle the trees. In a silent second Lucy could hear the grating of the Negroes' spades against the abrasive earth, digging for Grandma Bailey.

And then a razored scythe of lightning ran quick through the cloud, there was a blast of thunder, and heavy drops of rain started falling and spattering on the stones. Lucy and Mary began to gather up their things.

"It's going to storm," Lucy cried.

The Negroes digging Grandma Bailey's grave stopped working and started trying to erect a canvas and old Mr. Crocus ran scurrying, his back bent. And shortly long strings of rain came down. It began to pour thick drafts of rain, cascades of rain. The women ran squealing to the car.

They sat inside the Ford coupé, after they had snapped the isinglass window flaps, puffing and looking wanly outside. After a few minutes they took the napkin off the basket and began to eat the lunch, silently. Through the streaming windows they saw the Negroes digging under the dripping canvas which bellied in the wind, but the rain was flooding down through its holes. Already there was mud on their feet. Mr. Crocus was not to be seen anywhere.

Lucy and Mary watched the rain washing over the graves and saw the rain melting down the humps of earth. The rain was falling in torrents over all the graveyard. The sky was all mist and water now, and the little Negro shacks were dreary and dripping, washed gray. They did not even look lived-in, except for the forlorn face of a Negro at a window in a shotgun house, looking out.

They sat eating their good lunch—which seemed wrong, since they had done so little work to make it taste good; but still it seemed the only thing to do. In a while, Lucy looked out and said in a sad watery voice, watching the rain flood over the graves, "The good Lord bless all the dead," as if she had to make up to somebody for enjoying such a good lunch of chicken and pickled peaches. Suddenly she spied an armadillo lying ridged like a big spotted conch under a crape-myrtle tree. She quickly opened the flap of her window and threw the stone of a pickled peach at him. "Shoo!" she shamed it.

And then, in the melancholy rain, the two sisters saw the armadillo shaggle hideously and as if under guilt, dragging its ratlike tail, into the family plot. They were both silent and appalled. In a moment Lucy burst from the car and ran in the rain toward the family graves, crying, "Sooey! sooey!" But the armadillo was nowhere to be seen. She came back, drenched, and sat wet in the car. The noon whistle whined from the sawmill. They could not eat any more of the lunch now, yet they did not want to go.

"When we're gone, it doesn't matter," Mary finally said, quietly. "Think of all the things that come at night to a person's grave. Can't afford to think of it. We're protected somewhere else. Hold to the living, that's what. Laura's right not to come. Let's go, Lucy, to see about Laura. She'll worry about us in the rain."

They started the car and went back through the mud and steady rain to the house. As they drove into the yard to put the car under the big shade tree, they could see that some neighbors were there, on the breezeway. When they got to the door they could not believe what Mrs. Larjen, the next-door neighbor, in her bonnet that shook on her small trembling head, was telling them, that when she had come over to see Laura a little while ago she had found her slumped over the butterbean shells in her apron, and that when Dr. Murray had got to the house he said she was dead.

Lucy and Mary found her laid out on her bed and the neighbor women already sitting around her who looked, in her fresh death, more like her mother than ever.

Rhody's Path

Sometimes several sudden events will happen together so as to make you believe they have a single meaning if twould only come clear. Surely happenings are lowered down upon us after a pattern of the Lord above.

Twas in the summer of one year; the time the Second Coming was prophesied over the land and the Revivalist came to Bailey's pasture to prove it; and the year of two memorable events. First was the plague of grasshoppers (twas the driest year in many an old memory, in East Texas); second was the Revival in the pasture across from the house.

Just even to mention the pestilence of hoppers makes you want to scratch all over. They came from over toward Grapeland like a promise of Revelations—all counted to the last as even the hairs of our head are numbered, so says the Bible and so said the Revivalist—making the driest noise in the world, if you have ever heard them. There were so many that they were all clusted together, just one working mass of living insects, wild with appetite and cutting down so fast you could not believe your eyes a whole field of crops. They hid the sun like a curtain and twas half-daylight all that day, the trees were alive with them and shredded of their leaves. We humans were locked in our houses, but the earth was the grass-hopper's, he took over the world. It did truly seem a punishment, like the end of the world was upon us, as was prophesied.

Who should choose to come home to us that end of summer but Rhody, to visit, after a long time gone. She had been in New Orleans as well as in Dallas and up in Shreveport too, first married to her third husband in New Orleans, then in Dallas to run away from him in spite, and lastly in Shreveport to write him to go to the Devil and never lay eye on her again. We all think he was real ready to follow the law of that note. Then she come on home to tell us all this, and to rest.

Rhody arrived in a fuss and a fit, the way she is eternally, a born fidget, on the heels of the plague of hoppers. They had not been gone a day when she swept in like the scourge of pestilence. She came into our wasteland, scarce a leaf on a tree and crops just stalks, dust in the air. So had the Revivalist—as if they had arranged it together in Louisiana and the preacher had gone so far as to prophesy the Second Coming in Texas for Rhody's sake. She could make a man do such.

Already in the pasture across the railroad tracks and in front of the house, the Revivalist was raising his tent. We were all sitting on the front porch to watch, when we saw what we couldn't believe our eyes were telling us at first, but knew soon after by her same old walk, Rhody crossing the pasture with her grip in her hand. We watched her stop and set on her suitcase to pass conversation with the Revivalist—she never met a stranger in her life—and his helpers, and we waited for her to come on home across the tracks and through the gate. Mama and Papa and Idalou and some of the children stood at the gate and waited for her; but the bird dog Sam sat on the porch and waited there, barking. He was too old—Idalou said he was eighteen—to waste breath running to the gate to meet Rhody.

The hooded flagpole sitter was a part of it all. He had come in advance as an agent for the Revival and sat on the Mercantile Building as an advertisement for the Revival. He had been up there for three days when the grasshoppers come. Twas harder for him than for anyone, we all imagined. The oldtimers said he had brought in the plague of hoppers as part of prophesy. They raised up to him a little tent and he sat under that; but it must have been terrible for him. Most thought he would volunteer to come on down, in the face of such adversity, but no sir, he stayed, and was admired for it. He couldn't sail down his leaflets that advertised the Revival, for the grasshoppers would have eaten those as fast as if they had been green leaves from a tree. But the town had already had leaflets enough that read, "The Day of Judgment Is at Hand, Repent of Your Sins for the Lord Cometh . . ."

The first night he was up twas a hot starry night. We all sat on the porch till late at night rocking and fanning and watching him. There he was over the town, a black statue that hardly seemed real.

When the Revivalist first appeared at the house to ask us for cool water, we invited him in on the back porch. He was a young man to be so stern a preacher, lean and nervous and full of his sermon. His bushy eyebrows met together—for jealousy, Idalou told us after he was gone, and uttered a warning against eyebrows that run together. He started right out to speak of our salvation as if it might earn him a drink of water, and of his own past sinful life in cities before he was redeemed. He wanted our redemption, the way he went on sermonizing, more than a cool drink of water; but water was easiest to provide him with and best at hand, as Aunt Idalou said after he had gone. He was a man ready to speak of his own frailties and Mama praised him for this. He wanted to make us all free and purged of man's wickedness, he said, and his black eyes burned under his joined eyebrows when he spoke of this. When he had left, one of the children—Son—helped him carry the pail of well water to the pasture, and then we all broke into sides about who would go to the Revival the next night and who would watch it from the front porch.

When Son came back he was trembling and told that the Revivalist had two diamond rattlesnakes in a cage, right in Bailey's pasture, and that he had shown him the snakes. Then he told us that the preacher was going to show how the Lord would cure him of snakebite as a demonstration of faith. He had converted and saved thousands through this example of the healing power of the Lord, saying his famous prayer as he was struck by this rattling spear, "Hand of God, reach down and help antidote the poison of the diamond rattler of Sin."

Rhody added that she had already found out all this when she came through the pasture and stopped to converse with Bro. Peters—she already knew his name where we hadn't. Then she added that the Revivalist and his company—a lady pianist and three men who were his stewards and helpers—were going to camp in Bailey's pasture during their three-day stay in town and that at the last meeting, the flagpole sitter himself was going to come down and give a testimonial. She further informed us that she had taken upon herself the courtesy to invite Bro. Peters and his lady pianist to eat supper with us that night. We were all both excited and scared. But Mama and Idalou began at once to plan the supper and went in to make the fire in the stove to cook it with.

Rhody was not much changed—a person like Rhody could never change, just add on—as she was burdened by something we could not name. We all noticed a limp in her right leg, and then she confessed she had arthritis in it, from the dampness of New Orleans, she said. Her face was the same beautiful one; she had always been the prettiest in the family, taking after Granny who had been, it was a legend that had photographic proof right on the wall, a very beautiful young woman. But Rhody's face was as if seen through a glass darkly, as the Bible says. More had happened to Rhody during the years away than she would ever tell us. "Some of the fandango is danced out in her," Aunt Idalou said, and now we would all see the change in Rhody that we all hoped and prayed for.

Rhody was thrilled by the sight of the flagpole sitter. She said she was just dying to meet him. She told us that this town had more excitement in it than any city she had been in—and that included several—and she was glad she had come on home. She unpacked her grip and took out some expensive things of pure silk her husbands had bought for her, and there were presents for us all. Then she put her grip in the pantry as though she was going to stay for a long time but no one asked her for how long. In the early days, Rhody had come and left so often that her feet had trod out her own little path through Bailey's pasture and we had named it Rhody's Path. It ran alongside the main path that cut straight through to town. We never used it, left it for her; but if she was gone a long time, Mama would say to one of us who was going to town, "Use Rhody's Path, the bitter-weeds are taking it over, maybe that'll bring her home," the way mothers keep up their hopes for their children's return, though the weeds grow over and their beds are unused. Mama kept Rhody's room the way Rhody had it before she left for the first time, and the same counterpane was always on the bed, fresh and clean, the big painted chalk figure of a collie was on the dresser, the fringed pillow a beau had given her with "Sweetheart" on it, and the framed picture of Mary Pickford autographed by her, "America's Sweetheart." "She's got sweetheart on the brain," Mama used to say. She carried sweet-heart too far.

Anyway, the Revivalist took Rhody's Path to come to supper on. Around suppertime here came Bro. Peters and the lady pianist across Bailey's pasture on Rhody's Path, he tall and fast-walking, the little pianist trotting behind him like a little spitz to keep up with him. They came through the gate and onto the front porch where we all greeted them, and Rhody was putting on a few airs of city ways that made Idalou look at her as if she could stomp her toe. We were introduced to the pianist whose name was Elsie Wade, a little spinster type with freckled hands and birdlike movements of head. Miss Wade asked the Lord to bless this house and said that good Christians always gathered easily as if they were blood kin, which they were, Bro. Peters added; and we all went in the house, through the hall and onto the back porch. It was a late summer evening and the vines strung across the screen of the porch were nothing but strings after the grasshoppers had devoured them, but through the latticework of string we could see the distant figure of the flagpole sitter that the setting sun set aglow. Rhody kept wanting to talk about him. She said she thought he looked keen up there. Bro. Peters told that the flagpole sitter had been a drinking man, wild and in trouble in every county of Texas and Louisiana, until he was saved by a chance Revival Meeting in Diboll where he was sitting on the County Seat flagpole as a stunt for something or other. The night he came down to give himself to the Lord at the meeting brought wagonloads of people from far and wide, across creeks and gulleys to hear and see him, and many were saved. From that time on he gave his services to the Lord by way of the difficult and lonely task of sitting on a flagpole for three days and nights as a herald of the coming Revival. The flagpole sitter and the diamond rattlers were the most powerful agents of the Gospel and redemption from sin and literally brought thousands of converts into the fold, Bro. Peters told. Rhody said she was dying to meet him and Bro. Peters assured her he would make the introduction personally on the last night of the Revival.

We sat down to a big supper for summertime: cold baking-powder biscuits, cold kidney beans, onions and beets in vinegar, sweet milk and buttermilk, fried chicken—there was nothing green in the garden left after the grasshoppers had taken their fill. Idalou told Bro. Peters and Miss Elsie Wade that she had fed the Devil with some good squash that she had rescued from the grasshoppers but burnt to a mash on the stove; and Bro. Peters said that the Devil liked good summer squash and if he couldn't acquire it through his agents of pestilence he would come by it on a too-hot stove—but that he was glad the Devil left the chicken; and all laughed, Rhody loudest of all.

Afterwards we went to the porch and while Idalou

played the piano Son sang some solos, "Drink to Me Only," etc. But Rhody spoiled the singing by talking incessantly to the Revivalist. Then Elsie Wade applied her rolling Revival technique to the old piano that no one could talk over, not even Rhody, and made it sound like a different instrument, playing some rousing hymns which we all sang faintly because of our astonishment at the way such a slight little thing as she manhandled the piano as if it was a bull plow.

In the middle of one of the songs there was somebody at the front door, and when Idalou went she found it to be a man from Bro. Peters' outfit over in the pasture. He was anxious to speak to Bro. Peters. Idalou asked him in, but Bro. Peters, hearing the man's voice, was already in the hallway by the time the man entered. "Brother Peters!" he called. "One of the diamond rattlers is aloose from the cage." Bro. Peters ran out and Elsie Wade seemed very nervous, inventing a few furbelows on the treble keys as she looked back over her shoulder with a stiff pencil-like neck at the conversation at the front door. Her eyes were so small and glittering at that moment that she seemed like a fierce little bird that might peck a loose snake to death. Idalou invited her to wait in the house, though. "The diamond rattler is our most valuable property," Elsie Wade said, "next to the flagpole sitter."

All night long they were searching for the diamond rattler with their flashlights. We locked all the doors and stayed indoors and watched the lights from the windows. We started a bonfire in the front yard. There were fires in many places in the pasture. The bird dog Sam was astonished that we brought him in the house, but he would not stop barking; and Idalou said he would die of a heart attack before daylight if they didn't catch the valuable property of the viper, he was so old. It was a sinister night. At a certain hour we heard that the flagpole sitter had come down to help find the scourge of Sin. And then suddenly like a shot out of the blue Rhody jumped up and said she couldn't stand it any longer, that she was going out to help the poor Revivalist in his search for the diamond rattler. Everybody objected and Aunt Idalou said over her dead body, that Rhody's arthritis would hinder her if she had to run; but Rhody, being Rhody, went anyway. So there was that anxiousness added.

We all watched from the parlor window. In the light of the bonfire's flame we could see the eerie posse, darting here, kicking there, and we saw that the Revivalist carried a shotgun. The flagpole sitter had arrived in such a hurry and was so excited that he had not had time to take off his long black robe and hood that he wore on the flagpole, and his priest-like shape in the light of the fires was the most nightmarish of all. On went the search through the dark hours after midnight, and it seemed the Revivalist was looking for his Sin, like some penance, a dark hunter in the night searching for evil. And now Rhody was by his side to help him, as if it could be her sin, her evil, too. They seemed to search together.

We never knew, nor will, exactly what happened. When we heard the shot and saw flashlights centered on one spot, we knew they had found the snake; and when we saw them coming on Rhody's Path toward the house, the Revivalist carrying in his arms something like a drowned person, we knew it was Rhody. They came up on the porch, the Revivalist saying sternly, "Call the doctor, she was bitten on the hip by the diamond rattler and has fainted." He bit her bad leg.

They laid Rhody on the bed and Bro. Peters began saying his famous prayer asking the Lord to reach down and pluck the poison from his child. "The snake is killed—the flagpole sitter shot him," one of the men said.

It was Aunt Idalou who scarified the snakebite

with a paring knife and saved the life of Rhody until the doctor got there. Though she did it without open prayer, she prayed to herself as she worked on Rhody and used solid practical ways of salvation—including leaves of Spanish dagger plant in the front yard which Son ran and got, and hog lard. When the doctor got there he marveled at the cure and said there was little more to do except for Rhody to rest and lie prone for a few days. Idalou said she could count Rhody's prone days on one hand and Rhody commented that at least the snake had the common sense to strike her bad leg.

When the commotion was over and danger was passed, someone asked where the Revivalist was. He was nowhere to be found. In the early morning light, just breaking, we saw the pasture empty. There was no sign of anybody or anything except the guttering black remains of the bonfires. The flagpole on the Mercantile Building had nothing sitting on it. The whole Revival company had vanished like a dream . . . and had it all been one, the kind Rhody could bring down upon a place?

We hoped that would teach Rhody a lesson, but Aunt Idalou doubted it seriously. Anyway, Rhody stayed on with us till the very end of summer. Then one day there was that familiar scrambling in the pantry and it was Rhody getting her grip out. There was a mouse's nest in it. She packed it, saying she was going to Austin, to get her a job or take a beauty course she had seen advertised. When she had finished it, she told us, she might come back to Charity and open her a beauty parlor. We all doubted that, knowing she couldn't stay put for long in any one place, beauty or none.

We all kissed her good-bye and Aunt Idalou cried and asked the plain air what had branded her youngest child with some sign of restless wandering and when would she settle down to make a household as woman should; and we watched Rhody go on off, on the path across the pasture with her grip in her hand, going off to what, we all wondered.

"Well," Mama said, "she'll pull a fandango wherever she goes. But through some miracle or just plain common sense of somebody always around to protect her, with hog lard, or just good plain prayer, she'll survive and outlast us all who'll worry ourselves into our graves that Rhody will come to put flowers on, alive as ever." Rhody went out and took the world's risks and chances, but simple remedies of home and homefolks rescued and cured her, time and time again. She always had to touch home, set her wild foot on the path across the pasture that led back to the doorstep of the house, bringing to it across the pasture, from the great confused and mysterious world on the farther side, some sign of what had lately happened to her to lay it on the doorstep of home.

But with the world changing so fast and all old-time word and way paying so quickly away, she will have to correct *herself* in the world she errs in and by its means; or, in some way, by her own, on her own path, in the midst of her traveling. Surely we knew she needed all of us and had to touch us there, living on endurable and permanent, she thought, in that indestructible house where everything was always the way it had forever been and would never change, she imagined; where all, for her, was redeemed and put aright. Then, when she got something straight—what it was no one but Rhody ever knew—she'd gather her things and go off again.

"The sad thing is," Idalou said, rocking on the front porch looking at the empty pasture and the sad-looking path that Rhody took, "that years pass and all grow old and pass away, and this house will be slowly emptied of its tenants." Had Rhody ever considered this? And what would she do when all had gone and none to come home to?

But surely all of us who were listening to Idalou were thinking together that the path would remain, grown over and hidden by time, but drawn on the earth, the pasture was engraved with it like an indelible line; and Rhody's feet would be on it, time immemorial, coming and going, coming and going, child of the path in the pasture between home and homelessness, redemption and error. That was the way she had to go.

A People of Grass

He maundered about the city of Rome all day, mis-
placed. It was May, cold and dark and rainy, a bad
spring, a cursed spring. Blossoms were late, crimped
by cold and the pale touch of cold sun. He had left a
cold room on whose worn floor of ancient tiles were
sensual figures of faded crimson grapes and purple
pears that stung bare feet with chill, and where a wan
fire in a smoky fireplace did not warm naked flesh.
Here in this room he had risen in cold dawns to the
forlorn cry of swifts answering the toning of many
bells; and through a window he saw the sunless dome
of Saint Peter's that did not comfort.

In the late afternoon, a little before dusk, the skies
cleared as he was walking through the Borghese Gardens; and suddenly before him, in a green clearing
under great green trees, a flock of little girls from a

convent were there playing and singing on the cold grass. Four white nuns watched over them. Here in the gardens in late pale sunlight there danced and whirled all these little girls. He went closer and lay on his stomach in the grass at the edge of the dancing green and watched them. Some who had fallen or rolled in the new grass had the stain of green on their pink dresses. Some wore earrings they had made out of grass buds, or bracelets and necklaces woven of grass and early poppies; and watching them as he lay in the grass, there cleared in his mind an old confusion of a faraway afternoon, in one Maytime.

It was a memory of a sunny May afternoon in Woodland Park in faraway Texas with a soft wind in the great pine trees under which the school had made a clearing for the Grammar School May Fete. This was an enchanted day, and the brother's costume as the king of flowers was ready and his sister's as a poppy was finally made. The brother had a silver wand, a silver crown made of nothing but cardboard but dazzled over with silver paper, and the crown and wand lay waiting beyond his touch on top of the glass china closet that had been his grandmother's. (The brother kept the crown for many years, though the stars soon fell off and the silver burnished quickly; and lying there in the grass he wished that he might have it again, though it would change nothing.)

The sister's dress was a poppy, all of crepe paper, crimson and green, and for her head there was a little cap of an inverted poppy bloom with the green stem on it. Her costume lay spread on the bed in the extra bedroom that was to become her own when she was old enough to take it and no longer afraid to sleep away from the rest of the family. It was the most fragile dress, sewn with such distress by the mother who every day had spoken of the difficulty of it and how she thought she would never make it right if she had all her life to try. It did not last nearly so long as the brother's king's crown and his silver wand.

May Day seemed never to arrive but always hung at the edge of Thursday, until suddenly it was there, and there was the little family walking on the way to Woodland Park, the children in their costumes finally their own, holding hands and leading the way, the mother and father marching behind. The mother's eyes watched with a look of resignation the imperfect stem drooping on the sister's head as she walked carefully ahead. The brother could not see his crown, but he knew the sunshine was making it glisten, for he could see the way the silver wand, which he held very carefully as he walked, shone in the golden May Day light. The sister walked never so carefully in her life so as not to spoil her poppy dress, because her mother had warned her severely that the crepe paper would stretch out of shape or perhaps even "shatter," it was so ephemeral as any bloom, if she leapt or ran. The brother wondered how she could possibly dance the Maypole dance in it. She would have to do it very delicately.

At Woodland Park, a wide green slope on the banks of the Chocolate Bayou, there was a resplendent May crowd standing and walking about. There were gay lemonade booths decorated with colored papers, kiosks with colored lanterns swinging in the breeze, tent-topped stands where ices were sold, rustling in layers of Dennison paper and flags of ribbons. In the middle of the park was the clearing and in the center of the clearing was the grand Maypole, tall and strong, with its blue and white paper streamers drawn down and held in place at its base, waiting for each dancer's hand to take its own. The wind was trilling the whole delicate construction and there was such a silken rustling sound of paper and leaves that the whole frail world seemed to be made of leaf and bloom, all trembling and shining in sunlight and wind. How one hoped that the Maypole dancers would do it right, as they had been instructed through so many days of practice in the school auditorium. They had only one chance. Everything had the feeling of extreme delicacy and momentariness on this transient afternoon, an expendable moment of May, that rain could fade and wilt, wind could tear and blow away.

The sister found her assembling group of friends who were flowers: roses, tulips, lilies, and a few difficult wisterias. The mothers had done a good job of making the costumes, under the teachers' guidance. They had spent two tedious weeks all sewing delicate stuff in one of the classrooms after school.

As the brother was the king of flowers, he had to stand alone at his place of entrance, for there was no queen of flowers . . . why, one did not know or had not even thought of. The brother's costume was only a black suit, but his very first to own, coat and trousers, and a white shirt and tie; and that in itself was enough to make it a special day. But it was the crown and the wand that made all the difference. His task would be to move among the folded girls, all in a crowd, and gently touch each of them with his wand and so bring them up to bloom, while the lovely but somehow so deeply sad music of "Welcome, Sweet Springtime" played out from the piano. He waited with thrilling fright. He was second on the program, since the first thing was the entrance and procession of the King and Queen of May with all their court.

It began, and a boy walked out stiffly from the crowd, took his place by the empty throne and blew a fanfare as clear as sunshine on his bugle. He blew it right, thank goodness, and for the first time; and so there was no danger of giggles among the flowers who had not been able to control themselves during rehearsals when the bugle blurted and made no fanfare whatsoever. After the perfect fanfare, everyone was very quiet and the piano began. The court entered the clearing. The brother began to have a throbbing headache and to feel deeply sick. Out came the flower girls, the littlest, throwing rose petals to make a path for the king and queen; but the jester who followed, all in bells and pointed paper, kicked up the petals, against admonitions in rehearsals, and this was the first wrong thing. Yet how could he avoid tromping the blossoms? The brother grew sicker. Then the princesses came, teased, then the princes, the dukes and duchesses, and finally the king and queen, whom the school had voted for. The piano was rolling out its coronation march when the brother ran behind it, the music bursting in his head, and vomited there behind the piano, holding the crown with both hands to keep it from falling. He thought he might die from sickness and fright. But he felt better, now, though shamed, and he went back to his place. Now the court was seated, and without mishap, looking like a whole garden of flowers, and there was great applause. A pause, and then the familiar melody of "Welcome, Sweet Springtime," which had haunted him ever since they had begun practicing, filled the air. Suddenly all the flowers ran out into the clearing and fell to the ground around the Maypole, finding their streamers.

Then in a moment of blindness and exaltation, the brother heard his cue of music and it was time for him to come in among the flowers. He did not know what he did, but he remembered only a feeling of deep sadness and loveliness as he entered the clearing and moved among the folded flowers, touching each with his silver wand and bringing each up to flowering, all the beautiful little girls who so long ago vanished to many places and none ever so wild and shy again as that afternoon in a golden park of pine trees and flowers; and the whole Maypole began to open out like an enormous paper parasol. The brother knew when he came to the poppy that was his sister, for in an instant he saw, as he lowered his wand, that green fault in the stem which his mother had been so grieved at not being able to make properly, though the other mothers had said it would do and not to worry about it; and in the last weeks it had become the anxiety of the household. Once the mother even wept with despair over the stem and said, biting her lip and looking out the window, "I just cannot make it right"; and he had heard his mother and father speaking softly about it in the night. "It will be all right if you don't make it just perfect," the father had consoled her. "Children don't notice those little things." The brother and sister had been worried about the stem and wished, as they walked to school, that their mother could make it right. The brother even prayed for it at night, finishing his memorized prayer with "Lord help my mother make the poppy stem right." Then it was, at that instant, as he lowered his wand to touch it, that the little green stem seemed the fault in the household and a symbol of loving imperfection.

The brother touched with trembling wand the green stem on his sister's head, and he felt his sister shy at the glancing touch of it, saw her rise halfway as if in a spell and saw her trod a petal of her dress; and then he watched her stumble and fall, as if he had struck her with a burning rod.

He saw, in a mist of tears, a vision of his mother and his father and his sister and himself standing together in the clearing on the throne of May that was emptied of its royalty and where they had been brought to dock, ruiners of May, and the Maypole a twisted stalk of knotted paper behind them, casting shadow over them, his sister in her withered poppy dress and he in his suit with his burnished crown fallen down over his eyes like a blindfold and holding the silver wand that mocked him, his mother aggrieved and his father humbled; and he heard the thunderous laughter and soughing sigh, like a storm in the trees, of a vast crowd of May persons who, dressed in paper and leaves and petals, seemed to have come for a moment out of the trees and the grass and the rushes of the bayou that ran below the clearing, an assembly of judges and mockers and revelers, demoniacal and green and accusing. How cruel and how lovely was May, when everything was impetuous and passionate and merciless. And he could hear his mother's voice before the green jury, "I just could not make it right," and his father's, "We never had a chance, any of us, my mother and my father and my brothers and my sisters"; and the brother could feel his own wordless answer stirring in his depths where it would not for so long to come rise and be uttered.

The brother reeled back from his sister for a moment, but for some reason which he could not understand until many years later, until this moment when he lay in the grass of a foreign city on the rim of a little park where a crowd of orphan children played on the grass, he could not move himself to help his sister up. She had torn her frail paper dress; she was crying. The brother stood over his sister and his wand hung from his limp hand and dragged the ground and he began to cry, too, and there was a long interruption with the sister and brother crying, flower and king of flowers in the green clearing in the sunshine circled round by a world of faces, friend and stranger, all people of May, the music of "Welcome, Sweet Springtime" playing on, so very sorrowful now, it seemed a dirge of winter. Some of the flowers not yet brought to bloom by the wand could not restrain themselves from peeping up to see what had happened, and the whole garden was on the verge of shattering. In another minute a teacher had rushed out to help the sister up and motioned to the brother to go on. Yet he had not been able to help his sister come to flower, as he or nothing in this world could help his mother make the proper stem; and in that moment he knew certainly that no one ever could mend certain flaws, no mother's hands or brother's wand but some hand of God or wand of wind or rain, something like that, beyond the touch of human hands.

When the whole garden of flowers was in full perfect bloom, except for the blight of his sister whose dress was torn and one petal dragging behind her, and the Maypole opened out and trembling in the sunlight, the brother backed away from the clearing and into the crowd and found his way to hide behind the piano where he wept bitterly as it went on playing the sad springtime air. His throat ached, scorched with the lime of grief for his sister, for his mother, for this bitter time of May, and for his first suit and tie which seemed, then, to have something to do with some deep disaster of afternoon that even the crown and the wand could not alter or transform.

Behind the piano he wept bitterly in honor of more than he could know then. And he felt again as he had so many times before, already, in his very beginning life, that gentle blue visitation of a sense of tragic unfulfillment, a doom of incompleteness in his heritage, never quite brought to perfect bloom, as though its lighted way had been crossed by a shadow of error; and mistouched, stumbling, bearing its flaw upon its brow and shying for the touch of a magical wand, it could not rise, but struggling to rise it tore its flesh and limped into its dance.

Now the flowers were standing in their circle round the unfurled Maypole and in another minute they were dancing the Maypole dance, and the sister was there. The brother saw his sister dancing round and round, weaving her blue ribbon in and out without one mistake, pale and innocent and melancholy in her torn dress, dragging along with her while she leapt, as if she were a little lame, the broken petal of the dress that seemed already to be withering, and upon her forehead the blighted stem drooped and bobbled, grotesque and mocking like a little green horn on her brow; and the brother saw, as the whole May Fete witnessed, that surely the sister was the serenest performer of all the Maypole dancers, an aerial creature wan from early failure, touched with some pale light, skipping and singing softly in a visionary moment of unearthly beauty; and he, like her, in those moments, felt touched, too, by that wand of delicate heartbreak held by the demon king that lives in May, that momentary month that would pass and never come again until the world and all its flowers and grass had been touched and brazed by the summer sun, burnt by the frosts of autumn and buried under winter . . . until the Maypole's ribbons of paper would fade and the poppy dress shatter, the wand tarnish and the cardboard crown moult its silver stars.

Then, there in the center of the green at the end of this hazardous performance, all the dancers gone away, stood the enduring Maypole woven and plaited without one mistake; and in the empty clearing there lay upon the mown grass of May the lost petal from the poppy dress.

Now he was watching and hearing the little girls in the Borghese Gardens, again; but after another moment he was standing, and then, looking back at them, he walked away, touching with the fingers that had long ago held the magic wand the stain of grass on his white trousers. Bitter grass! The bitter water of the fountains of this eternal city is surely for the watering of grass, he thought. Bitter love of God that suffers for this majestic perishability that the planting wind blows over and withers! Bitter May! Bitter flesh, bearing upon it the ineradicable stain that tells the story of this oh great glory of flesh of grass!

In his alien room of ancient floor, round which the denouncing cry of the demon swifts whirled, he pondered the passing of early revelations, how they sink through the currents of years, their adornment dissolving away like petals of paper and pasted stars; and, at long last, shelled of embellishment and ungarnished, settle on the cold hard utter bottom and foundation of unalterable truth.

A Tale of Inheritance

A Novella

It is said—and true—that Wylie Prescott became the richest man in one part of Texas because of the accident of inheritance. But few people know the circumstances of his coming to power and wealth. That is the tale to be told.

One time were two sisters in a faraway county of Texas called Red River County, and they had little black beards. Their names were Cheyney and Maroney Lester—they were not twins but close to being that—and even when they were just young girls of about fourteen they had begun to grow a sprouting of black beard.

The way it began was that Cheyney's beard started to show first and then Maroney's. Cheyney was very distraught and particularly as she felt she might fall into bad light with her sister Maroney, whom she worshiped. But Maroney came to her and said quietly, "Don't worry, dear sister Cheyney, this will make no difference between us—and besides, now I will tell you that for a long time I have noticed the same thing slowly happening to me." The two sisters embraced and vowed they would stay together for the rest of their lives. This bond was stronger than death, although death kept it, too, and a very beautiful one to see, endearing the Lester sisters to all Red River County.

Red River County was a wildwood in those days, neighbors far pieces apart, scattered along the wide red river and upon the red land. Rain would leave red puddles in the gullies, and red dust stained the water in stock tubs. It had a wildness to it, too, this county, and where it rose to hilly places there were rocks and trees of hard wood, there where the water of the red river could not soften it. It was a beautiful wilderness and plain simple folks lived in it, and until the time of this tale, very few ever left the county and practically none that would never come back to it. This was all in about ninteen-fifteen.

Now there was a younger sister in the Lester family, ten years younger than Maroney and Cheyney; and her name was Princis Lester. Princis Lester grew along with her sisters and never spoke one word about the difference between her own aspect and theirs, though she took notice of it at an early age. She came to regard it as just the way they were, and there was no talk about it. But when she reached the self-regarding age of eighteen, and as she was slender and beautiful and chestnut-haired where her sisters' hair was of the coldest black, and they plump as two biscuits, Princis considered point-blank for the first time the plight that had befallen her sisters and thought death more desirable.

She said to herself, if this were to happen to me, I would just kill myself, looking at her face very carefully in the mirror. She drew farther apart from her sisters, though she had never been close to them, for Cheyney and Maroney seemed to hang apart in space from her, two little hemispheres joined by this isthmus of hair. Anyway, times were changing and Princis was taking her start in a new time. There was a new commissary up a few miles on the riverbank, and there were gatherings of young and old here, giving the chance to farm people to dress up and look at each other and adding one more to the opportunities of Sunday church and family meetings up and down the valley.

Princis asked no questions of her sisters about what she considered a fatal infirmity—they might have been dwarfs or albinos from the way she regarded them. Still, they were sweet and gentle, laughing little creatures, her sisters; and in the autumn she listened to them laughing in the apple orchard in their nunlike felicity, and she watched out her window at them sitting in the apple trees like charming coons throwing down the fruit. What did they have that she didn't? she asked herself at the dresser. A beard, she answered herself directly. The beard seemed to make all the difference, even that of blessed happiness. But she liked them, they were so loving with her, their own young sister Princis, they never once looked closely at her face to see if there was the slightest trace of beard, they never once mentioned it; and if she had been their sister and that close kin to them, Princis might never have noticed their peculiarity after being with them for a little while, the way other more distant kinfolks seemed not to notice, coming once and a while on Sundays to visit in the afternoons. Eccentricities that take on price and preciosity in cities become humble matter of fact in country places among country folk.

She yearned to go away to a city, to get her a job or learn to be a beauty operator, or take a course in something, as so many others were doing. But she waited. She finished high school and then her mother and father died within a year. She stayed on at home until she was twenty-five, yearning to run away. There was such a distance between her and her sisters, one she felt she could never bridge, never as long as she lived—she could not cross that bridge of hair. The neighbors and cousins were miles down the road and there were few callers besides them. She waited on. At night as she sat by the light of the glass lamp while her sisters played the xylophone in the parlor, she would scout her face very carefully in her hand mirror. Sometimes she fell into a kind of trance before the face in the mirror as though it put her into a sleep. Then the whole world lay only in the oval pool of her mirror.

One time at the supper table, Princis suddenly cried out to her sisters, "Stop staring at me!" and left the table. Maroney said to her, "Why, Princis, our own beautiful little sister, we were not staring at you." But Princis put on her coat and went out the back door. It was drizzling and December. She walked in the orchard under the dripping fruitless trees. "This means I must run away," she told herself, "or I will end up by harming my two sisters who mean no harm to anyone."

What was that little cry she heard in the dark orchard, some animal or what? She walked softly toward the cry and saw two lovely burning lights. Those were its eyes. She went closer toward the lights, and it was a cat that leapt away from her. She pursued it. Up it went, scratching into a tree, where its eyes burned like some luminous fruit growing on the bare branches.

"Kitty!" she called. "If you are wet and cold, come to me. I am Princis Lester and I will do you no harm. We can be friends with each other, if you will come on down."

She waited and watched the lights swinging through the tree. Then the cat came slowly down to where she stood and brushed a greeting against her. She picked him up, and he let her, and she felt how friendly his wet fur was to her hand, as though she had known it always. But its coat felt torn—it had been hounded by some animal.

Walking back toward the house with the cat, she said to it, "You have been lost in the cold rain and darkness. You had lost your way because you were nobody's cat and now you are mine; and what will I call you?"

In the house, Princis saw that the cat was a big black congenial male with cotton-eyes. She took off her new orange velveteen coat and wrapped him in it and took him into the parlor to show to her two sisters, and this would be an offering, too, to make up to them for what she had said at the supper table.

"Look here!" she said. "I have found a friend in the orchard."

Cheyney and Maroney ran delighted to Princis and the cat, whose head shone wet and black where it nestled in the orange velveteen. But the cat grumbled and spat at them and wanted to claw out to keep them away. Cheyney and Maroney drew back together, and Princis said, "He is just nervous," and took him into her room.

She sat down on her bed with the cat, dried him and brushed him with her hairbrush and said to him, "But what will I name you, because you are mine to keep." Some beautiful name, she thought. What beautiful names did she know? She could not think of any; but then suddenly a name breathed into her head, almost as though someone else were whispering her a name: Zamour! It was a lovely name she had seen on a poster nailed to a tree on the road and advertising a magician who would come to the commissary with a carnival that she never saw.

And so Zamour became Princis' own. He either stayed in her room behind closed doors or walked with Princis in the orchard where they had met. He stayed away from Cheyney and Maroney, never tak-

"And Zamour's future, too," Princis added. "For he will go with us."

Princis pinned a note on the hat tree saying, "I have eloped to Houston to get married and to make my future. Love, Princis."

Princis sent her sisters one postcard, showing a view of Houston looking north toward Red River County; and for many, many years there was no other word exchanged between them.

This was the time when people from small towns and farms were migrating to bigger towns and small cities, the time of change in Texas. Princis and Mr. Simpson moved into a small frame house in a neighborhood on Hines Street in Houston. The block of houses, called the Neighborhood by those living there, was inhabited by migrants from little towns, and a few were even from Red River County. These people had changed their style of living and slid into the pattern of the city. But oddly enough—for one would have thought she would be the first to change—Princis Lester did not alter, but from the day she settled there went on living as if she were still in Red River County. Something in Red River County kept her.

She did not dress up and catch the bus to spend all day in town, picking through Kress's or having a

Coke and sandwich in a department store luncheonette, gazing at women to see if their purse and shoes matched; nor did she spend her afternoons in vaudeville matinées at the Prince Theatre that bubbled dazzling lights even in the daytime; nor shop in Serve-Yourself Piggly Wigglys: she had a charge account at a little grocery store nearby where the man whom she knew personally reached up to the top shelf with a clamping stick to get her a box of Quaker Oats. "Whenever I get homesick for Red River County," one of the neighbors said, "which is less and less—it's all so changed, not like it used to be there—I just go look in Mrs. Simpson's house and feel I've been home to Red River County right on Hines Street in Houston. Why does she harbor home and past?"

When Princis raised the windows in her little house, she put sticks there to hold them up until Mr. Simpson explained to her that windows held up by themselves in the city of Houston. She had her Singer sewing machine and she pumped the pedal to make her print dresses with country flowers on them; she made her own sunbonnets and wore them in the Neighborhood and even in the house or when she swung on the front porch, like her sisters. She put her crocheted counterpane on the bed and her doilies, turned under her own hand, on the dresser and on the arms of the upholstered chairs to protect them.

Princis Lester's Houston behavior was an uncalculated change, among other changes, which at first surprised Mr. Simpson and then pained him literally to death. Princis kept herself from Mr. Simpson, and this took him by such surprise that he could not understand. She had shown him such a yielding eye at the commissary and in the hall under the hat tree. Still, for a while it was an excitement and a challenge to such a man as he, and he pacified himself by thinking about all Princis could give him, all the newly broken wilderness of future awaiting them both, when she was through her waiting. She turned, within the very first year, back toward her ancestry, and this in a world turning toward the other direction, so that such a new world could not support the change—it gave no ground to build upon, she might as well have made a house of mosquito netting; and against what weather could such a flimsy dwelling protect her? Princis became, in the Neighborhood, a curio left behind by a diminishing race, the last of the little country women, as if that race were finishing in her in a little house on a street in a city.

She seemed the last carrier of the bred-up aspects of a played-out species of large ears, small neat heads, faces no bigger than a coffee cup, dainty claws of hands with which to shell pea and bean, to cup a chick, to gather eggs one at a time and not to break any, to hang out small washings, dip one dipper of well water but not to draw a bucketful. When old Mrs. Graves first spied Princis Lester from her two-story boarding house across the street that once, when she and Mr. Graves first came to it from Benburnett County, was their home full of their seven children, she said to old Mr. Graves, sitting in his cane-back rocker in the one room they now lived in, "That new little woman in the Neighborhood will come to change and we will see her do it. Where are all the fine country women that once came to the Neighborhood, where have they all gone in the world? Something has changed them all away." The Graves house had been the grand house of the whole street which ran fifteen blocks between grammar school at one end and junior high at the other. On a corner, it claimed two lots, one a wide space of trees and with a small greenhouse, a chicken yard in the back. It had even had awnings. Now the cars of the boarders were parked under the trees and there was no grass there, only a sort of soiled dirt from drippings of cars; some blown-out tires were lying around, and on Sundays some boarders washed their cars there. The greenhouse was a wreck of glass, roof caved in and the stalks of perished flowers still in it. In summer, though, trumpet vines covered the ruin.

But in winter it was ugly to see. The servants' quarters were now rented to a woman from California who, at her age, was studying piano. Some nights it seemed she was trying to show off by playing the "March Slav" so loud for all the Neighborhood to hear.

Though Princis Lester stayed Red River County, Mr. Simpson took to ways of the Neighborhood and drew away from the house and from Princis. He was not a waiting man and he had waited beyond his capacity. Now it seemed to him that he had made a bad bargain at the commissary in Red River County, and he used these words one night to tell Princis Lester so. He started bowling two nights a week with the Hines Street Team while the wives sat in the boxes at the bowling alley and had their beer and cigarettes, yelling when the team made good strikes; or he went to baseball games and wrestling matches, or played dominoes in town somewhere; and he wanted Venetian blinds. More and more Princis was alone, except for one other thing she brought from Red River County and that was her friend Zamour.

In the evenings Princis Lester, in her straight-down country dress falling like a sack down her body, would stand on the front porch or walk up and down the sidewalk on Hines Street in the twilight and call to Zamour to come in. "Zamour! Zamour!" she would call, in a sweet song, until Zamour, plain country cat, would come dallying in on his delicate high hind legs and too-short front ones, so that he seemed to be coming down a ladder to his destination. Sometimes Mr. Framer, one of the neighbors and a policeman, when he was off duty sitting on his front porch cooling off with his bare feet cocked up on the banister, would mimic her and whistle back an insinuating whistle, until his wife, Mercel, came out of the house smoking her cigarette to tell him he ought to be ashamed. They were Rockport County people who drank their homebrew and fished on the jetties at Galveston on Sundays. They painted all the flowerpots red on their front porch and made a garden in their back yard with painted Roman-art bullfrogs standing on the rim of a fish pool, a goose, and a little elf sitting on a toadstool. Their garden was of city mode, azaleas and camellias; but there was always one row of onions and one of bell peppers and a little greens.

Time passed and Princis withdrew more and more from the city and from the Neighborhood. She would not answer the knock of visiting ladies from the houses in the block, and one in particular, a Christian woman from the Neighborhood church who said she brought greetings from the Married Couples' Class, and had a bob with a permanent wave in it. No one saw Princis Lester any more, walking in her sunbonnet to the grocery store in the late afternoons with Zamour following her and the two of them having their conversation. She and Zamour kept indoors. Neighbors watched her forlorn-looking house through their windows, ferns on the porch burnt up from lack of water, newspapers and circulars in yellow drifts on the porch. They wondered if she was sick or not. The men on the bowling team knew that Mr. Simpson had moved to the Railroadmen's boarding house in town and told their wives.

Then one afternoon there was suddenly the announcement of Zamour on the sidewalk, and sure enough at twilight the Neighborhood heard the call "Zamour! Zamour!"; and something was broken, like a long drought. They saw Princis walking up and down the sidewalk again. Her some sort of confinement was over, it was probably out of embarrassment or mourning at the flight of Mr. Simpson. Month after month, they followed this single daily appearance of Princis Lester at twilight, with only the calling of Zamour to let the Neighborhood know she was there, and her total silence and absence the rest of the time. "I think that's why she calls the cat so long and so sadly," one of the neighbor women said, "to let us know she is still there. For how else would we ever know, if it were not for the sign of the cat?" "And when she does come out, to call the cat," another said, "she looks white as a ghost. But that's because of the heavy powder she wears on her face, as if she'd fallen into the flour bin. Still, that's the old Red River County way: all caked powder, an inch thick, and no rouge."

One day Mr. Simpson fell very ill and was taken to the Southern Pacific Hospital. He lay there month after month, still a young man and sinking ever so slowly toward his death because of drinking. Princis Lester talked once to the doctors who came and made her let them in by crying out that it was a death message—and she said at the door, "About who, my sisters?" The doctors told her that her husband must have been drinking all his life, for he had a cancer of the spleen from it. Did she know? they asked her. "No," she said to them. "I never knew Mr. Simpson that well."

Princis would not go to see Mr. Simpson at the hospital. She wrote a postcard to Red River County—but not to her sisters—and asked her cousin, a twenty-year-old boy named Wylie Prescott, to come and try to get him some kind of job in the city and stay in her house until Mr. Simpson could die. He came—he was from the Prescott branch of the family, kin some way to her, her mother's younger brother's son, she remembered; and he had very little to say, or Princis heard little of what he said. She did not even ask him about Red River County. He took the back bedroom to have for his, though he never seemed to be in it.

The young cousin began a secretive life, the city provided him this opportunity, and he got a job driving a large dusty truck which he parked on Hines Street in front of the house at night. He made his own secret life right away, or found it; and sometimes in the humid evenings, now, the Neighborhood would see Princis and Zamour sitting in the swing on the front porch and the cousin on the front steps playing his guitar. The Neighborhood, living their ways, would all be in their houses: the Catholics on the corner in theirs, the one who had the big tomboy named Sis, in theirs; those in the rotting two-story Graves house in theirs—all the roomers in their hot lighted rooms, their cars parked in front of the house and their radios on at different stations—while the decrepit owners, Mr. and Mrs. Graves, sat pushed back into one room they lived in, with pictures of their seven children and their wives and children on the walls. The yards had been watered and the mosquitos had come, suppers were over, the oleanders were fragrant, and there was the sound of accelerating night traffic on the close boulevards. Tree frogs were in the trees, for there usually had been no rain for three months, and their song was as if the dry leaves were sighing. Then Princis Lester would stroll up and down the sidewalk, ghostly in her thick face powder, arms folded as if it were chilly, her felt houseshoes on, with bonbons of fuzz on the toe, calling, "Zamour! Zamour!" and there was the faint strumming of her cousin's guitar accompanying her little cat call.

It was her cousin Wylie Prescott who came in late one night and saw something, after sitting in his truck in front of the house with Mercel Framer, with whom he had become good friends, playing poker and drinking beer with her to keep her company because Mr. Framer the policeman had night duty. What the cousin saw was Princis Lester sitting in her bedroom by the low light of a little lamp, gazing like a statue into a mirror she held in her hand. Zamour was sitting on her shoulder watching and poised as if to catch a bird in the mirror. They did not even hear him come in. He watched Princis and Zamour, then shut the door very quietly and went on peeping through the crack. There she and Zamour sat, frozen in a spell of gazing. He went on to bed, thinking, "As long as they don't mess with my playparties I won't bother theirs."

When Mr. Simpson finally died, Wylie Prescott disappeared, so far as the Neighborhood could make out, for the truck was gone and no sign of him. Princis Lester took Zamour in out of the Neighborhood for good and they kept together in the little house very quietly, to wait for Mr. Simpson's pension. Every morning at five-thirty the faint click of the alarm clock, turned off now but still set at the hour when Mr. Simpson used to get up to go to the railroad yards, was like a little ghost living on in the clock. "Mr. Simpson is still living in that big ticking clock," she told Zamour. "But when his pension comes, we're going back to Red River County." She played a game with Zamour, to wait for the pension. "When we go back to Red River County, what shall we take with us?" Princis named things first—she would take this, and she would take that; what would Zamour take? Zamour did not seem to want to take anything, only looked up at her through his cotton-eyes, arched his back for her to put her fingers in his fur, and rubbed against her legs, shimmering up his tail. They had grown so close.

Most of the time Zamour had been so much like

a person, a beautiful, loyal, and loving person, that Princis had forgotten that he was just a mortal cat, and she talked to him, did nice things for him, making plans for him in Red River County. "We'll plant a little garden and have us some okra in it, have our cow, and there'll be a shade tree for us, when Mr. Simpson's pension comes and we go back to Red River county"; and she would run her fingers through his fur until Zamour would stretch himself long and electric under her caress. But when she would come upon him sprawled on the bed, involved in his frank bestial sleep, mouth gaping and wild teeth bared in his cat snore, she realized, passing to another room, that Zamour was just a dumb beast and could play no game with her, speak no conversation. "Why go back to Red River County at all?" she asked herself despondently. "He is no one to be with." Then was when she was so very lonely that she wished to see her sisters. She wrote a little letter to them and said, "Do not be surprised but I am coming back to the house in Red River County when Mr. Simpson's pension comes."

Her sisters were still there in the old house. There had been a few postcards exchanged during Mr. Simpson's illness and upon his death. What would they think when they saw her coming through the gate to the house, carrying Zamour and her suitcase?

Or would she surprise them, come at night without their expecting her, walk up the road hearing their xylophone music which they had played together for years, hymns and sacred songs and some songs out of their girlhood, but most of all "Beautiful Ohio," their best one. People passing the old house on the hill at night would hear the sounds of the xylophone and used to say, "Those are the sweet bearded Lester Sisters." She would open the door, the music would stop, and Cheyney and Maroney would run to her in their delicate bracelets of beard that seemed to hang from the tips of their ears and loop round their chins, and take her back; and the three of them would live the rest of their lives together there in Red River County.

But no . . . she could not. They were of another tribe, it seemed to her, almost as if they were of another color and language; they had their own ways, their own world—she was an alien there. There would always be the question in her mind, did they love her or did they mock her. It would only mean another waiting with the face mirror, to see if it would come to her, and with them waiting and watching, too—she was sure they would wait and watch, for how could they help it? I am not like them, I am not like them, she told herself; they make me feel so lonely and unusual . . . and she could not go back to them. She and Zamour would find a little cottage of their own near her sisters and they would live happily there on the pension. She would go to see her sisters once in a while, as the other kinfolks did, be nice with them, listen to their music, accepting their difference, as she had when she was young. The pension was what to wait for.

It was so long, her waiting. Now she and Zamour mostly sat in the upholstered chair in the living room facing the front door, waiting for the deliverer of the pension. She made a nice place of waiting there. She and Zamour would not go out for anything, for fear of missing the person who would come. Every morning as soon as the click of the shut-off alarm sounded in Mr. Simpson's clock, she would rise in a nervous haste and rush to her waiting place and begin to wait. Sometimes she fell asleep in the chair, waiting, forgetting everything but the waiting, and wake in the morning still in the chair; and go on waiting there. The chair took her shape, as if it were her body, and Zamour, who sat in his place on the back of the chair as if on her shoulder, had grown so nervous that in his waiting he had clawed it to its stuffing of straw and clotted cotton. But Princis had not heard or seen this. In the Neighborhood there was a wedding once, and Mercel Framer was shot at by her husband early one morning when he came home off night duty to find her in a parked truck with a stranger in front of his house, causing some scandal and commotion on Hines Street; and a baby of the Catholic family in the corner house had died—the funeral was held in the house and the cars were parked as far as the front of Princis' house. But she went on waiting, bridelike, in her chair, and never had a single notion of birth or death or scandal beyond this sensual embrace of the chair and the longing for the knock on the door as if a bridegroom would be there to come in and take her so full of anxiety and saved rapture. If she had to get up from the chair for a moment, the chair seemed to carry on the waiting for her, though it clung to her and was loath to let her go, they were so locked together. But she would instruct Zamour to keep his place and take over until she got back—and she came back to the chair panting, as if in desire, to plug herself savagely into it and be fitted tightly, shuffling henlike in it until she settled in a satisfaction on this nest of waiting.

If there was a knock on the door she would grow rigid and whisper to Zamour, "That's Mr. Simpson's pension, there they are"; and go to the door with a welcome ready—just to find a salesman of Real Silk Hosiery or Avon Products who, looking at her, stepped back as if frightened and went away. When the delivery boy had brought the groceries the last time—how long past?—and told her she could not charge them any more because they did not believe at the store that the pension would ever come, he stood away from her and stared at her. "They all must think I am crazy," she said to Zamour, and considered herself for a moment, then added, "because my face must show the secret waiting"; and went back to the chair.

Still the pension would not come, and she waited and she waited. What it was or how much, she could not guess; but the pension was what all railroad people talked about and waited for, and when it came, one beautiful morning, everything would be all right. How it would come or who would bring it she was not sure, though she imagined some man from the Government looking like Mr. Simpson in the commissary, when he was so fresh and full, arriving on her porch calling her name and as she opened her front door handing to her, as tenderly as though it were some of Mr. Simpson's clothes, a package with the pension in it.

One afternoon of the long time a rain storm began, and a neighbor knocked on her door to try to tell her there would be a Gulf hurricane in the night. When Princis spied the neighbor through the curtains she did not break her connection with the chair but sat firmly clasped by it and would not answer nor listen, seeing that it was no one bringing the pension. But the neighbor knocked and knocked until Princis went to pull back the curtain and glare at the woman to say "Give me my pension!" and Princis saw the woman draw back in some kind of astonishment and run away into the Neighborhood. "The Neighborhood is trying to keep the pension from us," Princis told Zamour.

The rain fell harder, and in a time the rain began to fall here and there in the room. She did not care. But the rain began to fall upon her waiting place, upon her and upon Zamour and upon the good chair. "They are trying to flood us out, before the pension comes," she said. She went to get the mosquito bar she had brought from Red River County and stretched it, between two chairs, over the upholstered chair, the way children make a play-tent; and over the mosquito bar she put a faded cherry-colored chenille bedspread she had made many years ago, just to make the tent-top safe. "This will preserve us from the Neighborhood," she told Zamour.

But where was Zamour? He had suddenly escaped the back of the chair in a wet panic. She managed to catch him, brought him back and wrapped him in her old orange velveteen coat with only his wet head showing; and huddled in the Chair under the tent, nursing Zamour, she went on waiting. The water was falling, everywhere now there was the dripping and streaming of water. She began to sing "Beautiful Ohio," but in the middle of the song she spied her favorite ice-blue glass lamp that she had had all these years, and she crawled out of the tent, leaving Zamour in his swathing and rescued the lamp. It was so dark. Would the lamp yet burn? She plugged it in the socket near the tent, and yes, it still glimmered pale snowy light and that made her warm and glad. She brought it into the little tent. She took up "Beautiful Ohio" again, right where she had left off. The tent began to leak wine-colored water and she remembered that old sweet red water in the gullies of home when summer rains came. There is my home, she remembered.

The wind rose and the rain poured down; and after dark, her blue lamp miraculously burning, a portion of the roof over the living room where she and Zamour sat, lifted and was gone. "What is the Neighborhood doing to destroy us?" she cried to Zamour. "They are tearing our house down and turning the Gulf of Mexico upon our heads." And she remembered the leering face at her window of the woman who had come with some threat and warning to her. "Still," she spoke firmly, "they cannot keep our pension from us. We will wait here." Through

coat of Zamour? She crawled on her hands and knees, the face mirror still in her hand, into the tent, muttering, "Lord, don't let the light of the little glass lamp go out"; and by the light of the lamp she held up the bronze mirror and saw in it her bearded face, and it bleeding, and the mirror cracked. Accompanying the watery sounds in her house she heard the low gurgling of Zamour somewhere in the dark drenched wilderness, like the sounds of a whimpering baby. She called out, "Zamour! Zamour! do not cry; come back to our tent, I am Princis, remember me; I will do you no harm." But Zamour would not come, he only wailed and sobbed his forlorn watery sounds of fear and alienation in the darkness. She humped under the ruined tent, in the sodden chair, and quietened. Then she whispered, "It is here, it has come, what is mine. Cheyney and Maroney, my two sisters of Red River County, I can come home to you now." And then the light of the lamp went out.

She sat in her chair under the tent in the wilderness. In her lost darkness, she tried to make up her life again like a bed disturbed by a restless sleep. What had led her to where she was, waiting for a pension that would never come? She could not name herself any answers—she would salvage Zamour.

She crawled out of her tent on hands and knees and the tent of gauze and chenille fell upon her like a net. She crawled on, dragging the tent, and hunted through the swamp for Zamour, ever so quietly. She might have been the quietest beaver. She saw two gleams—those were his eyes. She oared herself closer, closer, ever so softly. What was this lost and trackless territory she crawled through, it was like a jungle slough, it was not any place she had ever known, neither sea nor land, but a border-shore of neither water nor earth, a shallows where two continents divided. Zamour, Zamour, her heart begged as she waggled closer to his burning eyes, but her lips could not utter his name. Zamour, Zamour, something deep in her whimpered and bleated, as if it were cold, as though retrieving Zamour he might warm her like a collar of fur.

On her knees, she reached out to the two low gloamings and were they coals of fire that burnt her to the quick, or were they the eyes of a rattlesnake whose fangs struck her at her face? and she bouldered back, then reared up, bearlike, scrawling and pawing with her hands and arms to claw this fiend away. She heard the crashing of objects Zamour collided with as he escaped her. Was this wildcat clawing the world down upon her? She heard him making a sound that was familiar to her, somewhere, it was a ripping to pieces; and then she heard the burst of glass and the sound of spilling coins; and she remembered her lost waiting place with the chair and the lamp and the setting hen. Which way was this place, to go back to? Where was the light, where was the face mirror? Over there, she thought, still on her haunches. No . . . over here. And then she knew they were forever lost. She had no way, no sign to go by.

She lifted up, feeling now so light, like a buoy, and rising from her knees she sank again, at rest, like stone into the shallows where she was, another waiting place, as if she might from that moment on be a permanent mossy rock in these reefs and tides—of what geography? She breathed. It was all over. She gave it all up then. The tent was hanging from her as though she would carry it forever like a coat of hair. "I give up the lamp and the mirror and Zamour, and even the pension. I give up even the last thing," she said to herself; and, giving it all up to the last thing, she rested and settled, being this rock of nobody, no one she had ever known, renouncing all the definitions, the landmarks, the signs she had gone by to get to this nowhere in this dark bog of debris, on this lightless floor of the mud of her accepted eternity.

But what was that little cry? She found out two lights burning in the faraway distance. Some mercy ship is coming on some channel, she thought; what are those two mercy lights? It was an indestructible sign, lighting her memory back to an orchard on a frosty night and the sound of a cry and the glimmer of two eyes in a tree, and the meeting of two friends. *Zamour!* What was that watery music played out by the rain's hammering drops on broken glass but the tinkling little hammerstrikes of the xylophone . . . and oh her two sisters! She would survive in this dark world she sat in, she would start from there. For it was hers to begin with, to make her own. Something of her own had come to her and there was this to begin with: she was the sister of her two sisters, Cheyney and Maroney Lester and their own blood. If this darkness ever lifted and the waters ran away, if there was enough light to go by, she would try to find her sisters; and if there was no light she would go by darkness, rising out of these waters, and find her sisters wherever they were in this night waterworld and arrive there, steering herself home, to join them, crying, "See, I am your sister, Princis Lester." They would take her in, be so glad, there would be no more watching, no more waiting, *for they were sisters.* And they would live together in a home of warm felicity.

But Zamour uttered a kind of witch's cry again, from somewhere, somewhere, as if to call her to his claws again; and Princis Lester cried out in the darkness, "Zamour! I give up even you."

What time of night was it, because there was suddenly a bright light shining upon her and could there be a voice she heard saying, "Arise, shine; for thy light has come." Who, what had come for her? There were voices and knockings at the front door. They called her name. Why could she not answer? Then they beat upon her door and called her name, "Mrs. Simpson! Mrs. Simpson! Let us in!"

"My name is Princis Lester," she murmured, "sister to my two sisters in Red River County."

Then, how many of them there were, she could not tell—she had not dreamt there were so many survivors in the world—but enough to pound and kick against her door, calling her name louder and louder. She would not answer a thing, she could not move, until a loud strong voice called:

"Mrs. Simpson! Let us in! *Your husband's pension has come!*"

And at that call that echoed through the darkness, she began a lumbering crawl. Shaggy and dripping she buffaloed through the water, slowly slowly, dragging the immense weight of herself and the ragged tent over what seemed sharp rocks and broken shell of a sea floor, across the gravel and shale of the widest shore, slowly slowly toward the light; and found the door. Rising to her knees with her last gasp of strength, she pawed open the door and ogled into the dimming light and the blurring faces of what shining company of bright humanity that looked first like the young face of Mr. Simpson in the commissary, then like the faces, ringleted with hair, of her two sisters; and then there were no faces but it could be the guttering light of Zamour's eyes. "Hanh?" she murmured, with a look of mercy and salvation in her terrible tilted face; and this was how the Neighborhood caught her. Hanging from her as though it were the frazzled coat of a hounded animal was the rag of the chenille and mosquito-bar tent. A black shape shot through the door and into the Neighborhood, and it was Zamour.

That was quite some years ago; and for some years, quite a few, Princis Lester was in the Home, in the county seat of Red River County, resting. She could not tell anyone there what happened, or had no mind to—who knew which? She prinked her beard that wreathed her face like a ruff of titian down and took deep pride in it, it was her one interest. She seemed to be dozing at peace in it, something safe in a nest. There was a purity about her that everyone admired. She was the cherished one of the Home, quietly gleeful, considerate of others, craving no favors but getting them in abundance. She had a peculiarly enviable quality that made the others there

ing to him as they walked to the grocery store, for Zamour had that old dalliance in his gait. They saw him go on away, to somewhere; and he was never seen again in the Neighborhood.

Time passed, and with it Princis Lester, laid by her sisters to make three graves in Red River County. "Those are the graves of the bearded Lester Sisters," visitors to the cemetery remarked to each other. It was time for the next generation, and out of it rose the figure of Wylie Prescott to take his inheritance.

Wylie Prescott became a big figure of his generation in Texas, oil king and cotton king, cattle king and lumber king, and something important in the Legislature. He married a girl from a prominent old lumber family of Trinity County and added her inheritance to his. They had a daughter named Cleo and when she was sixteen took her to France and bought up a boatload of old, expensive antiques. While in France, Mr. Prescott went so hog-wild over French chateaux that he bought a whole one and had it moved, piece by piece, from Normandy to Houston, where it was put right back together again exactly as it had looked in some early century. It occupied a huge estate of many wooded acres, and Houston people drove by on Sundays and pointed at its towers topping the trees, telling each other that it was a French chateau from France. In it were all the French tapestries and coppers and cloisonnés, and among these were a once broken but now mended milk-glass setting hen, a golden thimble, and a cracked hand mirror, left behind to Wylie Prescott, heir to all Zamour's and Princis' waiting, with this tale hidden in them for no one ever to know, and Wylie Prescott's secret.

Though Cleo Prescott never asked questions about these old-time Texas relics that were now quite sought after as antiques, she showed more of a fondness for them than for any of the valuable French antiques; and when she fondled them, Wylie Prescott would warn her never to look in a cracked mirror because, according to the superstition, it would bring a curse of bad luck to women.

And that is the tale of Princis Lester and Zamour and the inheritance that followed them.

ter? He did not feel prepared, he had not been made ready. He could not bear a blade of grass, he thought, nor the sight of the thawed river across the yard that would, surely and irresistibly, crawl one day, like a reborn serpent, out of its frozen sheath.

Something between the man and his wife had gone stale and bloodless in the winter. They did not come to each other with any burning union; each stayed away to each, alien and suspicious and cunning, frightened to be touched, rankling at the approaches and the trespasses of each other. They had gone tired and rotten inside.

Because she had lost him somewhere in the long, sunless time, the woman in the house was wanting to take to herself anything vigorous and having surprise in it, anything to catch her up and bind her tightly to her place again. She had fallen loose and molty and not quick to any promise or challenge. Yet she defended herself against any signs of what she might be yearning for.

The whole house had the coldness and the lightlessness of languor in it. All the books seemed read and exhausted of being used. The stoves were scarred and sooted from long winter burning. There was nothing in the yard but stubble and bare boughs or the white burial of snow.

But on a night in late March there was a kind of

equinoctial turmoil in the world. It began in the afternoon with the triumphant entrance of a clattering wind that blew upon the earth and shined it like a chamois. At dusk the first rain came, sweet and cleansing; then scrawny snow fell, regretting the rain, like an emptying of the last few flakes of winter. In the earth and heavens there was the pitiful, almost embarrassing yearning and striving, turning and trial of an adolescent toward a vague and dubious call to fulfillment. There was clearly an agitation abroad, some kind of labor.

They sat at supper and resisted. They had had the wind at their doors and at their windows like something alien knocking to get in, and there had been the nervous rattle of trees and panes.

"If it is going to freeze again, I had better cover the pump," he said, and rose and went to the well.

She went on eating. Let him cover the pump, the well has gone dry, she thought.

After a while he came back and stood at the door. His hair was blown down and his face looked washed and bright. She thought him a stranger for a moment and she was frightened a little.

"Come outside by the well, Miriam," he said.

She got up and went outside with him, wondering what he had there at the well for her.

They stood, apart, in the terrible stirring of the

world outside. She would not venture to the well with him, but stood away, by a tree. He stood by the well with a faint arabesque of tenderness in his body. The unbearable scent of new rain seeped in the yard, and there was a quivering change shimmering over the well and toiling in the tree. Suddenly something had come. The old blood was trying to thaw like all the rivers in the land; there was a kind of sloughing time upon the world, a kind of shedding of old scabbiness, and they did not want it yet they were dumbly calling to it; they cared and did not care, were not sure, were troubled and uncertain. They stood apart, one under the tree, the other by the well. The smell of the washed earth seemed to turn them, "Turn, turn . . ."

Finally she said, "I'm cold and the supper will get cold."

They went into the house.

When they sat again, in a kind of shyness, they did not know what to do with each other. Their forks trembled in their hands and clattered faintly on the plates.

While she was washing the dishes, he suddenly looked at the window and saw a surprise there, like a gift left secretly.

"Look, Miriam," he called softly. "The geranium by the window is going to bloom."

She did not want to look yet, it had come too suddenly, without warning; and she stood over the dishpan not wanting to see anything, not wanting to go humble and bend to anything. But she took her hands dripping from the water and moved them with an infinitely subtle gesture of tenderness toward the geranium pot, as if she wanted to hold it a moment like someone beloved returned. For she saw, deep in the shadowy crevice between two limbs of the geranium, a cluster of little hairy pods gathered round together and covered with a frail green membrane. Slowly and ever so patiently, through a long, blossomless time, the geranium had waited by the window; and now it showed upon its body the sign of the change that had happened within itself.

He was watching her. But something called back her soiled hands to the water and she drowned them in the water again.

She stood with her hands hidden in the water as if she were trying to wash some stain from them, to cleanse them of some blight. Then she wanted it, willed it, and she looked again. There she saw it, the timid hesitancy of the beginning bloom, and she knew, now, that the same sign was in him. She saw him standing by the geranium, he was a little like new, himself, and she did not want to look him in the eyes, straight. But she looked again, this time trembling and defiant, and she saw the undeniable signal, the little, folded crimson annunciation, like a small horn to blow a reveille.

They had come through; and whatever it was that was stirring the earth outside had come into their house and, who knew, might come into them on the morrow, like a slow turning, like the bridegroom forth from his chamber and the bride out of her closet.

She went on washing the dishes, putting down a cup or a plate to be dried by him. And finally she said, as if she wanted to make an oblation to it, "Give the geranium a little water, Jim."

He felt as if she were unfolding, yielding ever so slightly to him. And when he sprinkled the water on the geranium she felt as if he were anointing her, and the blood in her hands quickened a little as she turned them round and round in the ablution of the water.

The Horse and the Day Moth

In Memory of Margo Jones

The waked dreamer was sitting on the side of his bed, head in his hands and staring at the floor, remembering his daydream and trying to order it, thinking how we see so much, know so much and yet are able to shape and tell so little of it all and that so slowly and with such pain. It was a hot summer afternoon in the great city.

Suddenly in the hot afternoon stillness and yet in

Reprinted by permission of *Mademoiselle*.

A newcomer would arrive, asking, "What's happened, what's happen—" and stop cold when he saw, over a shoulder or through an opening in the crowd, the still pile of black animal on the wet pavement. The horse's head was stretched upward and its teeth were bared as if it were neighing and its mane lay wet over its neck. It seemed twice as large as any animal, this horse, in its death. The buildings around seemed smaller. He had turned and walked away. Where to go, how to be? he wondered.

As he walked away there flashed in his mind a little scene of two summers back, in a garden in Texas in the summertime, when he had gone home for a visit with his mother, who was very ill and would have perhaps no other summer ever beyond this one. She was able to sit in the garden and so they sat under the afternoon trees in a wooden porch swing hung from the branches. She was speaking of flowers flourishing in the garden under her own hand. There was the sound of a hammer in the background, and he thought how always in the summertime there had been the sound of an unseen, remote carpentry in this neighborhood of small, clean wooden houses, some repair going on, someone mending his house in the fair days before winter came. His mother was naming the flowers to him again for the hundredth time, speaking of their eccentricities, of their hardships under the sun or too much rain, of the "perennials," of this one "that turned out to be white though I bought it for a red"; and how the grandchildren in their games had run through the round flower bed "but, anyway, the seeds came up in their footprints." "The flowering garlic has already run up seed, and it so early," and he looked to see it sure enough speared on top with its own seed as though it were at that moment "running up" seed as he looked at it.

It was a sad time and yet a very serene time and, feeling this, he got up to go look at the Louisiana daisies that had been brought many years before from Shreveport when an aunt came from there to visit and that were purple beyond any purple. He saw this: on a blossom there lighted, out of nowhere and as if out of his mind, in a gentle glee, a little lion-faced butterfly the size of a bee. There was a shagginess about this moth—it was, really, a little day moth—a mongrel quality it was; and yet it had a fierce face of lions and leopards and was the color of those. This was the kind one had always been able to catch easily, they were so tame. Here was this little thing, still in the world and still over these flowers, waiting for pinched fingers to catch. One had somehow thought they had all vanished, this scrubby, ordinary little race of butterfly! He easily or who would raise it again; though he knew the fragility of his violence and the delicacy of his ferocity. But he saw, now in his room, that a balance was struggling, that a shape from outside, in the world, and inside, in a dream, was at work. There is a link, he knew again now, between the happenings of the daily world and the dreaming mind that holds its hidden images. It was as though life were unfolding on either side of a partition, a wall.

Now he held the dream as close as another body in his bed; and now there was a joining, as in love. We cannot believe, he thought, how all things work together toward some ultimate clear meaning, we cannot believe. Human life is at once in a conspiracy to prove us of small or no end, and a conspiracy of incidents and images to lead us to a beginning again. There is the constant, gentle and steadfast urging of the small, loyal friendliness, the pure benevolence of some little Beginningness that lies waiting in us all to be taken up like a rescued lover and lead us to a human courage and a human meaning. The rest is death: murder (self or other), betrayal, violence and cruelty, vengeance and crimes of fear. But the little Beginningness is in all of us, waiting.

In his dream he had seen his mother standing half in the doorway of the house, in darkling light, in the attitude of an early photograph he knew of her, her hair bobbed and graying, for she was so ill, even then, calling out to him and his sister in the yard where they had drawn a hopscotch in the dirt: "Come on in now, it's darkening." And when they had gone in, he and his sister, they had found the house filled with the darkening and no answer to the call but the low, gentle, echoing cry, "Come on in now, it's darkening."

Now all in his room there was the hovering presence of the day moth.

seemed no resolution or pacification of this hidden strife.

What had happened to these people? He heard ringing accusations, warnings of reprisals, threats of vengeance. This one voice, that of an older man (was he the father?), said it was going to leave, was going to pack its bags and get the hell away; this other voice, a woman's, young and shrill (the daughter's?), said it despised all the rest of the family and would be glad when it could move to an apartment of its own; and still another, that of a young man (the son?), declared that all life was filled with liars and cheats and wished it could cross the ocean to another country, any country, and die; or get on a long train and travel away, forever. Finally, the oldest voice of all, a flat old woman's (the grandmother's surely), delivered over the other voices declarations of doom and godlessness and hopelessness, said its long, tired life would never end in peace.

At noon each day there seemed to be a kind of truce, for silence hung over the cursed family below him. Then there was not a sound. Perhaps they had murdered each other and all lay dead and quietened. But around three o'clock the strife began again and rose in the sunless air of the deep and desert chasm between his building and the next so that the echo in this hellish canyon between two brick sides of buildings where windows opened out onto a bleak damp hole was like that of damned souls. Then the city seemed breathless and suffocating, without mercy or hope, and was he placed here to live out an eternity of hatred and accusation and self-doubt on the rim of a pit of despair from which hollow voices wailed and resounded? His work desk was fixed against a little window that opened onto the chasm, and the savage attacks from below rose and echoed into his room and hung over him as if to mock his work. He tried hanging double folds of blankets at the window to seal out the sound, but this only created a more sinister echo of muted crying and clashing and shrieking of voices. Once he spoke to tenants who lived below the damned family, wanting to find some sharer of his haunted days and nights. But to his surprise they said they heard nothing but an occasional scraping of chairs or the traffic of feet, that was all.

One day it was so unbearable that he was filled with despair and left his room in the morning. He walked the streets in the rain and sat in the park in the rain, looking at human faces as if he had forgotten there was any humanity left in a race of haters and accusers. Away from his tormented room, he saw that his nights and early mornings, when he lay in his bed and heard from the pit the hollow rising for him, for the world? Was this the difficult and verily impossible-seeming miracle wrought at last, at so long last? Might it be the beginning of something new, of change toward better, toward hope?

After large limousines had opened their doors and received the wedding and borne it away, he crossed the street and ascended the steps. There were petals of flowers lying there. Inside, as he began to walk up the four dark flights of shabby stairs where he had once imagined shapes of terror lurking and expected to encounter at each turning some face or figure of anguish and doom, he saw here and there on the stairs the petal of a rose, the blossom of an anemone. He approached the apartment of hate and heard not one sound from it. Had they gone away, if ever they had existed, the accursed family? When he passed their door he saw a wreath of white flowers fixed there. Now he knew that the beautiful wedding had come from the house of violence.

He went into his room where the very air seemed becalmed and he opened his little window and listened and felt peace over the chasm that had held despair. Then he sat at his desk and began to prepare himself for some day that would soon come for him, an event of glad tidings, some fulfillment of wish, reward, a day or a night of beautiful sensation, some abstract gladness, some sight of loveliness, the sunshine lying upon his floor, the birds of spring lighting the Trees of Heaven beyond his back window, and the air and light of springtime filling the winter chasm of despair.

ABOUT THE AUTHOR

WILLIAM GOYEN was born in Trinity, Texas, in 1915. He went to school and college in Houston, taking B.A. and M.A. degrees at the Rice Institute. Following college he taught literature at the University of Houston for a year, then enlisted in the U.S. Navy, where he served four and a half years on an aircraft carrier in the Pacific.

After the war he settled in New Mexico, where he began writing. His first novel, *The House of Breath,* was published in 1950. Mr. Goyen was awarded the MacMurray Award for the best first novel by a Texan, and a Guggenheim Fellowship in 1951. In 1952 his second book, a group of tales and stories called *Ghost and Flesh,* was published. In that same year he was granted a second Guggenheim Fellowship. After a year in Italy and Switzerland, he returned to New Mexico and began writing *In a Farther Country,* published in 1955. Since that time he has been living in Ottsville, Pennsylvania, and in New York City, working on a play, *The Diamond Rattler,* which had its premiere at the Charles Playhouse in Boston in the spring of 1960.

Mr. Goyen's fifth book, a novel entitled *Half a Look of Cain,* is in progress and he hopes to have it finished in early 1961.

His stories have been printed in most major magazines in America and Europe; and he is a frequent reviewer for *The New York Times Book Review.* He has been teaching literature at the New School in New York City for the past three years.